For our children Olivia, Callum, Nathan, Drew and
Heather, and the child within us all.

Prologue

Angus froze, as out from the corner of each eye, on either side of him, he could see two huge hunting dogs baring razor sharp teeth towards him. The man that had shouted walked into view and caused a chill to run down Angus' spine. He motioned the dogs to sit beside him, blocking the lever. The dogs still bared teeth that would surely rip Angus to bits in seconds. He had never been so scared in all his life!

"So Angus we meet again. Just what did you hope to achieve here?" He paused for an answer and since Angus did not seem able to speak, he continued, "Did you think that I was stupid? Did you really think that you could just waltz in here and take my dragon?"

"Look Angus, look at your friends. They cannot help you now" He advanced further. "I've been watching and waiting for you. I knew you would come. Did you not stop to think, when you found my front door open, that it was a trap?" he mocked as he grabbed Angus roughly by the arm. The man pushed him forcefully and released the hold. Angus, finding himself off balance, fell to the floor. As he looked up he thought about what had happened in the last couple of weeks and how he had got here…

The Secret Society of Dragon Protectors

Chapter 1

'The Dragon Boy'

It was the middle of July and the long and eagerly awaited summer break loomed on the horizon. Like many children, Angus looked forward to the freedom of imagination that a release from the school routine would bring. He wondered what he might do these holidays and was hoping for some adventure.

At school he always had his nose in a book and didn't join in with the other boys playing football or daring each other to do stupid things to see if they could get away with it. He simply wasn't interested. He was not your typical eleven-year-old boy and in truth, Angus was a bit lonely. There was no-one of his own age living close by and his parents were always too busy to drive him anywhere. He looked ordinary enough but unlike most boys at his school, he was not into sports all that much. Angus had blond hair that he kept slightly untidy and even though he looked a bit on the puny side, he was actually quite wiry and strong. This was mainly due to the fact that he rode his bike everywhere he went.

Towards the end of term he was caught doodling in his history book instead of listening to Mr Masters. The teacher had reached the end of his tether with 6C and took out his frustration on Angus whose inattention happened to be the last straw, not that he was usually in trouble.

"ANGUS MUNRO," Mr Masters bawled across the classroom. "WHY ARE YOU, NOT PAYING ATTENTION? What could be more interesting than my lesson?" He strode up to the boy's desk and held up the drawing. It was of a splendid dragon. "So you prefer to draw silly little dragons, rather than learn about World War Two." Mr Masters had addressed this to the class and received the titter of laughter he was looking for. The teacher honestly thought the drawing was rather good and very detailed, but obviously could not say that out loud. This public embarrassment of Angus just gave the rest of the class ammunition and an excuse to ridicule him. This wasn't the first time. After class all he got was 'dragon this' and 'dragon that' and was generally taunted about being into dragons. He didn't mind really and secretly liked it, as at least he was getting some attention. He would just smile or laugh and when they realised they were not getting a rise from him, they moved on to the next victim.

For as long as he could remember, right back to when he was a very small boy, Angus was fascinated by all things dragon. Much in the same way that boys latch on to cars or planes, trains or motorbikes, soldiers or dinosaurs Angus' small world was dragon-filled. To Angus dragons were not scary, mythical beasts personifying evil like some storybooks portrayed. Nor were they the stuff of nightmares. To him they were gentle, protective and largely misunderstood creatures. His favourite bedtime story from an early age was 'The Dragon's Tale' given to him by his Gran. Every night, before he would go to sleep, his Gran would read it to him. In fact she read it so often that they both knew the words off by heart and she didn't need to hold the book at all. He followed the old-fashioned text with his finger and that enabled him to correct the storyteller if she tried to make it a bit shorter or forgot some of the words. Not that his Gran would ever do that, she had had all the time in the world for her only grandson. His Gran had lived with Angus and his parents for a little while and it was a very happy time for him. She was his best friend; someone to share secrets with and she always encouraged him in whatever he did. His Gran was old-fashioned in her ways but very cool at the same time. She always had time for him and they did everything together. It was his Gran that taught him to read and to ride his bike. Even when he did something naughty the old woman was never cross with him, she just had a way about her that made him feel sorry for the thing that he'd done. He could never bear to disappoint his Gran.

Angus' interest in dragons did not diminish as he grew; indeed it flourished, and he spent hours making fine pencil drawings of the mythical beasts in all their magnificent scaled splendour. Even though he was eleven, Angus still had his beloved 'Dragon's Tale' on his bookshelf, a little dog-eared now but occasionally he would get it down, dust it off and rekindle that warm and glowing comfortable feeling which a childhood memory can bring.

Angus spent a lot of time in his Gran's care, as his parents were too busy to do much with their only son in the early days of setting up and managing their Kleanware business, which they ran from the family's converted garage. They were totally absorbed in selling environmentally friendly cleaning products and gadgets that supposedly made peoples' lives easier so that they could spend more time with their children. That part was rather ironic as Angus' parents were so intent on making money that they sometimes forgot they even had a son.

They were quite oblivious to his loneliness, and as far as Angus was aware they made plenty of money. He never wanted for anything; at least, nothing of a material nature but all he wanted was some of their time. They worked very hard in their widespread area and did everything themselves; distributing catalogues, making up the orders, delivering them in their Kleanware van and they were always on the lookout for new customers.

Although Angus' Gran had passed away quite peacefully a couple of years ago, he still treasured the book which she had shared with him so often and it brought back many happy memories of the dear old lady whom he loved so much. Angus took the old book down from the shelf and started to read.

The Dragon's Tale

It was a curious thing. The old dragon ride had stood outside Mrs James's sweetshop for longer than anyone in Piggleston could remember. Generations of children had sat on the much loved and well-worn green scaly back whilst their parents were inside the shop unencumbered, buying sweet treats for after tea. Many a melting ice cream had dripped down that long green neck and no-one had ever fallen off the dear old creaky dragon.

Put a coin in the yawning slot, hold on tight and away you go. Rocking to and fro, anywhere your imagination would care to take you. The creaking from the old mechanism could be heard all along Piggleston High Street and that sound was as familiar as the cracks in the pavement. When it stopped, you would open your eyes and know that strong arms would be there to lift you down.

That day, someone had carelessly said,

"The old dragon is looking a little shabby and old-fashioned. Isn't it time we replaced it with a modern shiny red fire engine?"

Nobody saw the once gleaming eye squeeze out a solitary salty tear. Luckily it plopped onto the pavement for if it stayed on the dragon's face it would surely make her rusty!

"I wonder what it's like up there in the clouds, and what Piggleston looks like from the sky," the old dragon mused. "If only I could get off this plinth and see for myself..." It was almost as if the dragon had heard her destiny.

"It's now or never," she sighed and she drew herself up with all her might and began to rock to and fro. There was nobody sitting on her green scaly back to steady and steer her. Faster and faster she rocked furiously to and fro and smoke started to stream from her blazing nostrils. Her once fierce eyes suddenly glowed with new life and, with a loud snort and a swish from her mighty forked tail, her great green webbed wings started beating. She was at last free from her plinth and she rose magnificently above the rooftops of the shops in the High Street.

Onward and upward the dragon flew. One – two, one – two, beating her great green webbed wings, in and out, in and out. If you have ever seen a dragon in full flight you will know what a truly magical sight that can be, but how could the dragon fly solo? Nobody had slipped a coin into the yawning slot on the plinth. Perhaps, just perhaps if you wish for something with all your might, you can really make it happen!

Higher and higher she stretched her wings and soared, at last looking down on the tiny town where people resembled little dolls and the cars looked like toys. Even the clickety-clack railway track looked like a zip from way up there, and the trees were green lollipops; the dragon's favourite colour!

After a while, the dragon's great green wings grew tired and she knew her adventure was almost at an end.

"If I finish up in the scrap yard tomorrow, I shall end up a happy dragon," she thought. "I have seen beyond my plinth." She steadied herself, gathered all her strength for the descent and gently glided down to land on her plinth, folding her great green wings around her.

Mr James was just coming out of the sweetshop with an oilcan and a pot of paint labelled 'dragon green' in either hand. Her wonderful flight was unseen by Mr James or indeed by anyone in Piggleston.

"Here we are old girl, we'll soon have you smartened up and running smoothly – no more talk of replacing you; what a terrible thought!"

Now if you happen to go to the town of Piggleston and you see a green dragon on a plinth outside a sweetshop, why don't you go up and say hello or better still, put a coin in the slot, climb onto the green scaly back, hold on tight and close your eyes, wish your best wish and dream of flying with dragons? Maybe, just maybe with a swish of that mighty forked tail and an unfurling of those great green scaly wings she will fly away with you for another adventure. You never know!

Angus put the book back up on the shelf and smiled as he remembered how his Gran had been this stern woman who never seemed to miss a trick.

It was now two days into the school holidays and Angus was already bored. He'd already shoved endless

Kleanware leaflets through the letterboxes in the neighbourhood. He wanted to find some adventure story to escape into and knew just the place to go. Monday just couldn't come quickly enough.

Getting out of bed around eight he dressed hurriedly and went down to the kitchen. He looked at his Mum and Dad, already there and; as usual working at the breakfast table. His Mum had blonde hair, which he inherited; she had sharp features with a warm friendly face. His Dad had brown hair and was starting to go a little grey and thin on top and his face was more oval. He had a nice smile when he used it but most of the time he was too serious for smiling.

Angus was named after his Grandfather. He never knew him as he had died before Angus was born. He was told that the old man was originally from Scotland but had lived in England for most of his life. Angus was not a common name in England, but he liked it as it made him different somehow. He was possibly the only person named Angus in the county.

"Hi Mum! Hi Dad!" he said loudly. He received the usual grunt that came from his Dad, who didn't even bother to look up from the laptop.

"Hello dear," said his Mum glancing up from the paperwork she was doing.

"What are you going to do with yourself today?" she asked with slightly feigned interest. He had no sooner started to answer her when she started to look back to her figures.

"Well I thought I would burn the school down today!" he said not too loudly.

"That's nice dear."

Shaking his head he ate breakfast cereal quickly before he jumped on his bike and rode into town. He parked the mountain bike against the warm red brick wall of the local library. This was one of his favourite places in the whole world. He loved the haven of silence and the way tens of thousands of printed words from down the years hung expectantly in the air. The familiar musty smell of old books greeted him as he pushed open the heavy glass door which closed behind him with an alarming 'swoosh', earning a deadly raised eyebrow from Miss Puttick, who had been librarian since time immemorial. Like his Gran, she was a very stern looking woman, though Angus suspected she was not quite as old as he had once thought. It seemed she never smiled and with the way she dressed, so prim and proper, meant she was not very approachable. Angus waved a soundless 'sorry' and breathed in the atmosphere, eagerly anticipating choosing an adventure story. What Angus actually found on the 'new acquisitions' shelf of his local library would however transform his school holidays and indeed his whole life forever!

He headed for the junior section and could almost hear the books vying for his attention on the higgledy-piggledy shelf; 'Choose me, choose me' they seemed to dare him. Miss Puttick had unusually neglected to tidy the junior section after the last assault by a herd of holidaying children. She always kept the library shelves in apple pie order and neatly regimented, but for now, she was totally engrossed in the general knowledge crossword in her newspaper. Nonetheless, whilst chewing her pencil as she pondered four across, she kept a sharp eye on Angus. Now, thought Angus savouring the moment, what to choose? Pirates, soldiers, boy wizards... Out from the corner of his eye, Angus spied an old greenish leather bound book entitled 'Dragonalia' within the 'new acquisitions' section. He lifted it down carefully from the shelf as it looked quite delicate.

"That book is for reference only; it's not to leave the library," Miss Puttick hissed fiercely, looking up from her crossword. Overenthusiastic boys with sticky fingers handling delicate library books with lots of lift up flaps and envelopes ripe for tearing were her worst nightmare.

"I will be really careful," he replied politely.

Angus could feel the burning of her disapproving glare as he carefully sat down at the reading table with his find. He ran his hand over the scaly fabric cover and marvelled at the fabulously detailed illustrations. This small hardback book was a dragon enthusiast's dream come true and he spent the whole morning pouring over its contents and absorbing every fragment of information about dragons and their ways.

It took him about a week of daily visits to the library to read the handwritten pages from cover to cover and several times over. Angus made copious notes in a spiral bound writing pad as Miss Puttick looked on. He scribbled away and from time to time she would sidle over, pretending to tidy a shelf of books allowing her to have a look over his shoulder. She could not help herself commenting on his notes and sketches.

"My! You are really getting good use from that book young man," she said in an unusually friendly manner. Looking up at her and smiling he replied enthusiastically,

"Yeah I know. This book is fantastic! I wish I had a copy but the bookshops don't stock it."

This was true, as he had checked in town and also checked the Internet during a visit to the library earlier in the week. He couldn't find any reference to the book anywhere or strangely, even the name of the author.

Angus gladly showed her his notes and sketches, explaining that he learned that dragons were attracted to shiny objects; rather like thieving magpies. In particular they craved gems and some metals, and they would go all out to acquire them. Dragons picked up jewels by rolling on them and the gems stuck to the underside of their belly, which is the only non-scaly and therefore most vulnerable part of their body. This jewel hoarding was a mixed blessing as it gave them additional armour. In medieval times men had used precious stones as bait to lure dragons into captivity or destruction. Angus learned that they were shy but usually trusting creatures, especially when being bribed with jewels, making them easy prey.

At home he tried to talk to his parents about his discovery but they were not terribly interested. They just wished he put more effort into his schoolwork but if he was being honest, Maths, Geography and History didn't capture his imagination in the same way that dragons did.

After the first week of the school holidays Miss Puttick began to think of Angus as the Dragon Boy and she began to soften towards him and looked forward to his daily visits. He was the only visitor to the library who bothered to talk to her, beyond the usual brief exchange over library tickets and overdue book fines. Libraries were not usually conducive places to start a conversation.

Angus and Miss Puttick struck up a curious kind of friendship that can sometimes quite surprisingly happen between two very different but equally lonely people of different generations. Angus for his part was surprised by the librarian's interest in him. He had always found her to be a bit fierce until he had taken the chance to get to know her properly. He didn't have his Gran around anymore and his parents were too wrapped up in 'saving the planet the Kleanware way' to pay him much attention, so he took to Miss Puttick as she reminded him of a younger version of his Gran. Angus was anxious to share his newly found knowledge with someone and as his parents continued to be too busy to even feign any interest in what they called his 'dragon nonsense', Miss Puttick seemed the most likely candidate. Although she was no dragon expert she was enchanted by his excitement and solemn belief; she had even relaxed her 'total silence' rule a little so they could converse in hushed whispers when the library was empty. Some of the boy's enthusiasm rubbed off on the lonely librarian and touched her heart. Angus told her about 'The Dragon's Tale' of his childhood and he asked her if she had ever read it. She hadn't; so he fetched it in the very next day and sat watching her tired and lined face soften and mellow as she read the well loved tale. With a tear in her eye at the end of the story, she looked up and asked Angus,

"Have you ever been to Piggleston to find the dragon in the story?"

Angus didn't realise it was a real place and shaking his head in disbelief he replied "No."

"Well I can't say I noticed one but like your story says, you never know," she smiled in reply.

Miss Puttick herself had been to Piggleston many a time and vividly recalled Mrs James' sweetshop with its endless jars of rhubarb and custard sweets, rainbow sherbet, cough candies and all the other old-fashioned sweets you could possibly imagine, but she did not remember ever seeing a dragon outside on the pavement. But then again Miss Puttick did not have any children and so was unlikely to notice such a thing anyway.

The next morning when Angus arrived at the library, he felt a little bit disappointed that there wasn't more to 'Dragonalia' as he had absorbed all the information from between the two covers and he couldn't help wondering,

'What next? What can I do with all this?'

Miss Puttick saw that he was struggling for more information and had a surprise for him that she thought was sure to put a smile on the Dragon Boy's face.

"Angus, what do you make of this?" she said. As he walked to the desk she pushed an old, somewhat torn and faded piece of paper across the counter.

Angus looked at her smiling face and then back to the paper. He could barely make out the title and screwed up his eyes to try to decipher the unusual script. It seemed to be a pamphlet and along the top in stylish handwriting, it read;

'Societas Arcana Draconorum Custodorum
The Secret Society of Dragon Protectors'

Chapter 2

'Finian Tek'

Angus could hardly believe his eyes! Miss Puttick mistaking his silence for something else said,

"Well it's only a bit of old paper but..."

"No. It's magic! Honestly. But where did you get it?"

"Dragonalia was a gift. It was not purchased directly from a publisher or a bookshop and maybe that is the reason you could not find it," she explained and encouraged by the smile on his face she went on. "It was donated by a strange visitor... a man... I can't recall his name though... He came into the library some years ago and said that he had written it." She paused as if lost in that memory before continuing, "I had put the book away and forgotten about it, and it was only when my memory was sparked off by the crossword clue I was stuck on the other day. 'Where was St George alleged to have killed the dragon?' that I remembered the donated book. I got it out of the cupboard, found the answer I was looking for and decided to put it on the shelf."

Angus hung on her every word as she told him about how she had acquired the book.

"I was making sure that it was all in good order and that all the flaps and inserts were intact when I found this" she continued, pointing to the pamphlet. "It was hidden and I very nearly threw it away as it seemed beyond restoration and repair and would take an awful lot of tape to mend it. Throwing away the written word is actually against my nature so instead I tucked it in the back of my desk drawer, until today."

A smile as big as a Cheshire cat, spread across Angus' face. Seeing the pleasure on the young lad's face, she pushed the old pamphlet towards Angus

"You take it home and keep it. I have no use for it. In fact it seemed rather bizarre to me and it's not really part of the book."

"Thanks" he whispered, not taking his eyes off the paper for a second.

"Hopefully you will find it interesting since you are becoming such a dragon expert!"

Angus raced home, shut himself in his bedroom, flung himself on his bed and began to read…

Societas Arcana Draconorum Custodorum

 The Secret Society of Dragon Protectors

Congratulations on finding this document. You have discovered something that will change your life and your attitude to the world around you. Since you have managed to find this hidden document within the book of 'Dragonalia', I can tell that you have assimilated all the information in the book about dragons; know about the properties of Dragonore and how to use it; and that you are therefore the type of person I am looking for. The type of person who not only likes to read and learn about dragons but is also determined enough to go that little bit further to gather all the information that they can obtain.

Firstly let me tell you about the History of this Society. The Secret Society of Dragon Protectors or SSDP, used to have members from all over the world. These members were dedicated to the protection of the great beast commonly known as draco; dracon or dragon as it is known in English.

The Society was founded hundreds of years ago, in fact it is not known exactly when but it is believed that George the Knight, reputed to have slain a dragon, was the first of the dragon protectors. Dragons were dying out and would now be extinct if the Society had not been formed and intervened on their behalf. Down through the generations many ancient families have dedicated themselves to the society's motto, beliefs and oath. Unfortunately these noble bloodlines have dwindled, died out or had younger generations turn their backs on the duties passed down to them from their ancestors.

The society's motto is "Magnam Bestiam Servare," which can be found on the society's coat of arms and means 'serving the great beast'.

The beliefs of the society's founders were that the dragons needed to stay hidden from man until such time as was deemed safe enough for them to return to the world at large. Dragons possess vast amounts of natural magic and have abilities that man can only dream of. One of these abilities is to transform into another shape and hide from the eyes of those who would do them harm. This defence mechanism has served them well for centuries but is not enough to completely protect them, thus the need for the Society.

The Oath of the SSDP is simple.

A dragon protector shall;

Dedicate himself to the motto and beliefs of the SSDP.

Respect the SSDP rules of secrecy.

Never misuse the SSDP.

Always put dragons before himself and his own well-being.

Only pass on the legacy to those worthy of the task.

Having read this pamphlet you probably think that it is some elaborate, practical joke. I cannot blame you for this. You are also asking yourself what all of this has to do with you. Well if you have read this far then you are indeed as interested as I would like and expect you to be. The whole point of this document is to attract the attention of any would-be dragon expert and potential recruit for the society's dwindling numbers. Indeed that is why I, Finian Tek, wrote 'Dragonalia' in the first place. Anyone not worthy of the task would see the book as pure fantasy and dismiss it at that. You however have not and it is you I am interested in.

If you would like to know more about the SSDP then you must write to me at the address below. Please give as much detail about yourself as possible. Tell me why you want to know more from me and what you know about dragons.

If I think you are the type of person I am looking for then I will contact you and arrange to speak to you further. Once again my congratulations on coming this far and hopefully we will meet at the soonest opportunity.

Yours in faith and trust,

Finian Tek
Long Reach
Lower Dinton
Wellshire
United Kingdom

Angus blinked in disbelief. The crumpled and musty pages were timeworn and fragile but Angus soon found himself engrossed in the beliefs of a group of men, led by one Finian Tek, the last modern member of an ancient secret society sworn to defend and protect dragons from a corrupt and violent world. Finding this pamphlet, and together with the knowledge he had gained by reading 'Dragonalia', Angus was further convinced that dragons were still in existence today! He recalled that the only way a dragon would now communicate with a human, was if that person possessed a piece of…what was it called? He

The Secret Society of Dragon Protectors

flicked through his notes. Dragonore – a precious rock that enables a dragon to recognise that human as a potential friend. He looked up at the dragon picture he had on the back of his door.

"Wow! Now if I could only get my hands on a piece of that!" he said to himself.

The aim of the SSDP was to protect dragons at all costs, and to keep their whereabouts secret. He looked again at the address of the SSDP and the name of the man, Finian Tek, whom Angus now knew, was the author of 'Dragonalia'. He was inviting him to get in touch with him by letter. At last! Someone to talk to about dragons! Somebody who could answer all his questions and tell him more about the fabled beasts, a dragon expert!

Angus wasted no time in tearing a piece of paper out of his History book and writing to Mr Tek at the address on the foot of the pamphlet, using as it turned out, the back of the dragon sketch he drew in History. He licked down the envelope, jumped down the stairs and stuck a stamp on it. A thought struck him, like a bolt out of the blue. Supposing there was a piece of Dragonore with the book when it was given in to the library! It did seem to be a sort of 'handbook' so just maybe... He had to go speak to Miss Puttick at once. As he reached the front door he heard his Mum shout from the office-cum-garage,

"Sort yourself out some lunch! I'm going out to the bank and your Dad's busy with orders." She clearly had no time for him right now. Angus didn't answer but instead shot out of the house, slammed the front door and pedalled furiously back to the library, only stopping to put his letter in the post box. He got there just as Miss Puttick was locking up for Saturday's half day closing. He panted and spluttered out the gist of his discovery and asked,

"Was there anything else with the 'Dragonalia' book other than the old piece of paper?"

"Only a bit of old rock in a matchbox" said Miss Puttick. "I found it at the bottom of the bag it came in. I had kept it for ages but I threw it out yesterday when I opened the drawer to get the paper out for you."

"Where did you throw it?" asked Angus urgently, his heart sinking as he knew the dustmen had already been. The banging and crashing of the dustbins had woken him up early.

"I threw it in the rose bushes over there. It seemed to be just a stone so I returned it to the earth" she said proudly. Miss Puttick pointed to a neglected rose bed, and at once Angus dived to his knees and started scrabbling about in the weeds, prickles and dirt. He fumbled around for a few seconds with Miss Puttick looking on very puzzled by his actions.

His fingers tightened around a small stone, dull and uneven, looking like nothing more than a clod of earth. Surely this could not be Dragonore, which was supposed to be shiny, precious and highly sought after by all dragon protectors? He rubbed it vigorously on his shirt and as the hardened mud fell away he could see the faintest glimmer of aquamarine! Feeling warm to his touch it shone brightly, reflecting the light with a fierce intensity almost as he imagined a dragon's eye to be and he enjoyed the warm weight of it in his hand. He brought it closer to his face, wondering at its unearthly properties and was sure he could feel its power. The mineral seemed to shine brightly for a moment and then it lay still and inanimate once more.

"What ever is that, Angus?"

"It's Dragonore and it allows dragons to recognise you as a friend," he replied.

She looked at him for a moment and was thinking that she should really tell him that dragons were not real. However the look on his face as he stared at the stone made her smile and say instead,

"Well that's good. All you need now is a dragon."

He tucked it in his pocket, thanked her and rode home in a daze.

That evening, Angus' usually busy parents surprised him by actually having a full conversation with him. Well, a sort of conversation which was the type where they talked and he listened.

"There's a two day market which offers an important sales opportunity and your father and I feel it's a great chance to show off the new range of Kleanware products as well as have a short break. So we thought we would go to Flourmill Cottage next weekend. We can't think of anyone to leave you with so you'll have to come with us but we're sure you will be able to find something to amuse yourself."

Angus was amazed to be included in his parent's plans but also rather dismayed. He really didn't want to go anywhere away from home just now; not when he was so involved with his dragon project, and anyway he was expecting a reply to his letter from Finian Tek of the SSDP any day. He stomped off up to bed and his parents thought him decidedly ungrateful. He knew what a 'weekend away' with his parents meant though. When they were not on the market stall they would be in the pub and he would be left outside it with lemonade and packet of salt and vinegar crisps for hours on end. It never occurred to his selfish parents to actually do anything with their only son; it was always assumed he would just occupy himself. Angus supposed he was lucky that he was happy in his own company and just got on with it but even so, it would be nice come first, just once. He sometimes wondered why they had a family at all as they were both so wrapped up in their Kleanware Empire. When he was a small boy, the Munros had involved Angus in painfully embarrassing demonstrations of stain removal liquid and such like at country fairs. That was his parents' idea of a family holiday; driving around the British Isles promoting Kleanware products! He had no reason to think this weekend away would be any different.

"We won't be going far, only somewhere local for a couple of nights, a change of scenery!" his Mum shouted after his retreating back.

Angus spent Sunday in his room, it was raining and the library was shut. He lay on his bed studying the Dragonore taking in every detail of its surface. All he could do was think about dragons now. He even dreamt about dragons! He always did but now his dreams seemed to be more real. Next morning Angus casually enquired.

"Any post for me?" and was disappointed to see only the familiar returned Kleanware envelopes on the sideboard.

He went back to his favourite refuge, the library. Looking for sympathy he told Miss Puttick about the proposed weekend away.

"Where is this stupid 'Flourmill' place anyway?"

Miss Puttick listened wisely as she had her own opinion of Angus' parents but didn't share them with the boy.

Directing Angus to the 'local maps' shelf of the library she said.

"Why don't we find out?"

Her knowledge of the locality was much better than the boy's and she thought he might change his mind when he saw where his parents were actually taking him. Together, the librarian and the disappointed boy poured over an Ordinance Survey map and found the location of Flourmill Cottage. It seemed to be just on the outskirts of Piggleston. Suddenly Angus' eyes lit up. He had just realised that the place in the story, which he had thought of as imaginary until Miss Puttick had told him differently, was very close to where he was staying with his parents that weekend! Maybe this trip was 'destiny' after all and would not be quite as dull as he first thought. He resolved to take the Dragonore and the pamphlet and go to find the dragon of his favourite childhood story to test out a theory about hibernating dragons. He left the library a whole lot happier than he had entered it.

The rest of the week could not go quickly enough and at last Friday arrived. The only thing that he was disappointed about was that he had not had a reply to his letter yet. Of course Angus spent most of his time at the library re-reading 'Dragonalia' and he even made a copy of the old pamphlet that Miss Puttick gave him.

Miss Puttick struggled with her crossword. Just what was the capital of Liberia? At least she was in the right place to look up the answer. She fiddled absentmindedly with the matchbox on her desk, which was far too useful to throw away. It had the picture of a castle on it amongst a mass of strange blue flowers. The name of the castle was on the box as well, but she hadn't taken much notice of it. With a librarian's mentality she filled it with paperclips and elastic bands and other useful bits and pieces.

Arriving at Flourmill Cottage, Angus helped his parents unload the van and they carried the stuff inside the low-beamed cottage, which was to be their home for three nights. Typically his parents had brought too many boxes of Kleanware products so as not to miss a sales opportunity. True to form, his parents didn't seem to be planning to spend much time with their son and already the mobile phone was ringing.

"Phew this is thirsty work son. Listen, your Mum and I are off to the 'Merman's Trousers' for a quick pint," his father announced as he finished the call.

"Remind me later, that's two boxes of 'Save the Rainforest' toilet roll for the Smithwicks on Monday... Now will you be alright on your own for an hour or so son?"

"I'll be fine," Angus declared as his Dad looked around for his keys and wallet. "I might just familiarise myself with the High Street, that's all."

Looking round at the Kleanware products his Dad said "Now you won't get up to any...."

"No I promise I won't get into any trouble Dad. Honest!" Alone in a cottage full of eco friendly washing up liquid and detergents, wow what fun! Did his parents really think that his only source of amusement would be messing around with Kleanware products?

Pleased to be on his own at last and hardly able to contain his excitement he set off along the High Street and soon found the sweetshop looking just as it did in the illustration of the story; rows of jars in the window containing every kind of old fashioned sweet you could imagine, to be weighed out and sold by the quarter – no metric conversions in Mrs James' sweetshop! And then, he spied it, there, right outside the window on the cracked pavement; the dear old dragon ride which seemed as familiar to Angus as his own face. Nobody was around and the dragon ride stood quite still and solemn. He didn't really know how to address a dragon so he walked up with an outstretched hand, much as if he were approaching a horse or a dog, showing that he meant it no harm. He reached the plinth, his palms quite sweaty, not sure of what might happen. He felt a bit silly as he took in every aspect of the dragon's face and noticed that it was quite freshly painted, dragon green of course!

Angus felt that perhaps he was a little too old to ride on the dragon, although a coin was burning in his pocket. Then he realised it wasn't a coin at all, but the piece of Dragonore. He took it out and realised it was radiating heat and glowing. His concentration on this was broken as he realised his father, red-faced and smiling, was strolling up the High Street.

"Ah there you are Angus. Come on I'll buy you a bag of rhubarb and custard sweets. I've got the munchies so I'm foraging for chocolate, your Mother's gone on ahead to make tea."

Angus reluctantly left the dragon and trailed after his Dad back to the cottage, brightening slightly at the thought of buttered crumpets. As he walked up the street he gave a slight backward glance towards the shop. Just for a second he thought he saw one of the dragon's ears move slightly. No, it couldn't be. He must be imagining things!

Chapter 3

'The Dragon in the High Street'

The next morning Angus rose early, before his parents had emerged from their bedroom. He shouted an offer to get a local paper for his Dad and quickly sped back to Mrs James's. There the dragon stood, silent and solemn as before but he could have sworn that one of the dragon's feet was in a slightly different position on the plinth than from yesterday; claws pointing inwards.

Once again the Dragonore glowed and warmed in his pocket. Glancing along the deserted High Street he moved closer to the dragon's face. Still not sure how to address the dragon, his heart was beating fast in his chest and he thought it would burst. Was he perhaps going bonkers? Did he really expect this piece of painted metal to come to life? Angus began to have doubts but with one hand on the stone in his pocket he gingerly touched the nose of the ride. This was quite brave if he really was expecting the dragon to come to life, as it may have ignited him in flames or bitten his hand off in the very least!

No he was being silly… Nothing was going to happen… was it? He cleared his throat and tried speaking

"H…h…Hi I'm Angus, I'm sure you can hear me."

No reply or any other indication of life seemed to be forthcoming. He tried again.

"I saw your slight movements and changes of position."

After a few more seconds of silence Angus decided he was being silly and was just about to walk away when he heard what sounded like a female voice, quite breathy and creaky, whisper,

"What do you want?"

He looked about to see if anyone was playing a joke by speaking to him from a hiding place; but no-one was in sight, apart from Mrs James in the sweet shop and Angus could only assume it came from the dragon itself. He bent his head closer to the dragon and it gave a slight wink. Angus was so amazed that he shot back, overbalanced and literally fell on the pavement landing with a thud on his bottom. He stared, open mouthed at the dragon and then picked himself up. He backed away slightly, still refusing to take his eyes off the scaly face, bumping straight into Mrs James who had come out of the sweet shop to see what all the early morning commotion was about. In his fright and astonishment Angus ran all the way down the High Street and only stopped when he got round the corner. Panting and gasping he tried to catch his breath. Crikey! How could that be? He couldn't believe his ears! Or his eyes! Perhaps the Dragonore had retained its ancient powers and he could see through the dragon's disguise! He could not believe that the dragon had actually spoken. To HIM! Angus! Suddenly he felt rather foolish for running away. He hurried back to the shop and went in to apologise to Mrs James.

"Oh now don't you worry about that my dear. Just as long as you are alright."

She asked him what his favourite sweets were, offering him a couple to help calm him down after his fall. He assured her he was fine and then heard,

"Psst…get some cough candy can you? I haven't had one of those for years!"

Mrs James was still staring at him from the other end of the counter, waiting to hear his choice and clearly oblivious to the voice Angus had just heard. Too stunned to do anything else, Angus found himself asking the shopkeeper politely for a couple of the orange twisty sweets with the fiery taste. He thanked her again and went back outside ready to approach the dragon again.

"Mmmm, cough candy, my favourite, please do share!" said the breathy voice. An amazed Angus popped a sweet in the dragon's painted mouth.

"So the Secret Society of Dragon Protectors were, right," he murmured and the dragon pricked up her ears.

"The SSDP? What do you know of those?" she whispered.

Angus was about to launch into an explanation when the dragon interrupted,

"Not now though," she added giving a slight nod in the direction of an approaching toddler.

"Come back later when we can talk properly." Angus moved aside and a young child was lifted onto the dragon's scaly back and a coin fed into the yawning slot on the plinth. 'Hold tight' instructed the girl's father as he disappeared inside the shop and the dragon started rocking to and fro much like the scene described in the story. Angus pretended to scan the notice board outside the shop offering all kinds of second-hand goods and gardening services. He listened longingly to the creaks and groans of the old mechanism so familiar from his childhood book. How he would love to have a ride, but at eleven he was obviously far too big for such a thing!

When the coin was spent and the young rider lifted down, Angus noticed that the Dragonore had stopped glowing and burning in his pocket and the dragon ride stood quite still, silent and solemn as before. He couldn't wait for time to pass so he could come back and carry on his conversation with the dragon. He could see that the High Street was starting to fill up with people and that the square was busy with market traders putting up stalls, as it was market day. Soon the place would be busy with locals and tourists so he knew he would not get another chance to speak to the dragon. For now he entered the newsagents, purchased a Piggleston Herald as he was supposed to do, and hurried back to the cottage before his parents missed him. 'Like that was about to happen!' he thought.

He spent most of the day either in the cottage, outside the pub, or hanging around the market. His Mum and Dad would start conversations with stallholders, trying to make new contacts and giving out business cards. They even went as far as bringing stuff to the more interested stallholders and showing off the Kleanware range first hand. The market was only here once a month and they pitched their products to everyone they could, showing off all the things they had brought with them. Angus didn't really mind about this as he had got to meet the dragon and if they did this every time the market was here he at least would have an excuse to come and visit.

Every now and then Angus would catch a glimpse of the dragon; he was sure it was a she, but always the sweet shop was busy and a small rider would be laughing on the back of the dragon ride. Angus' parents decided they were going to the pictures that evening but he politely declined their invitation to join them. He really did not want to watch some boring film and was anxious for them to go out as soon as possible. Angus assured them he would be fine and picked up a paperback as a decoy, implying he was going to spend the evening reading.

As soon as he saw his parents retreating backs disappearing down the road, Angus waited a minute or two and then ran to the High Street; the precious stone firmly in his pocket. The sweetshop was closed and a security light from within bathed the dragon in a half glow. Once more he approached the dragon hand outstretched so as not to alarm her. He felt the Dragonore warming in his pocket and he touched the painted nose.

"It's me, Angus, can you hear me?" he whispered. Encouraged by the feel of the ore glowing in his hand, he took another step forward.

"My name is Pyrra" replied the dragon. With a hint of mistrust in her voice Pyrra asked,

"How did you know I was here, and how do you know about the SSDP?"

Angus explained how he had come to possess the pamphlet of the Secret Society of Dragon Protectors and how he wanted to find out how he could continue the work of that small group, and he revealed the glowing Dragonore. The dragon blinked and in a soft, creaky feminine voice she spoke;

"So that is how you found me."

She pondered Angus' story for a moment and deciding he was trustworthy she explained,

"There are not many of us left now. We have been hunted down the centuries and mankind has done us great harm. We have to protect ourselves to survive. You must be a true believer to be able to see through my alter-shell, and you also have Dragonore, our precious rock, see how it glows! We dragons love bright and shiny stones and this is the greatest treasure of all."

She went on to explain about the Great Hibernation, and how, in fear of extinction at the hands of humans, the few remaining dragons had hidden themselves in dragon themed objects. She herself had always loved children and therefore became a child's plaything more recently made into a dragon ride.

"What became of the others?" asked Angus.

"I have no idea. The problem is that I think that most of us have forgotten how to re-awaken or lost the will to do so. I don't know how it came about with me, but I awoke, stretched my wings and flew unobserved around the skies above this town. I'm a bit rusty though and need a bit more practise."

"Oh I know about that!" said Angus "I read about it in your story!"

"There is a story about me? Oh how marvellous!" the dragon preened. Angus had many questions to ask of his newfound friend and the two chatted quite companionably unseen by the villagers, late into the night. Angus reluctantly felt it was time to go.

"Do you think next time you fly you might take me with you?" whispered Angus fearful that he might be pushing his luck just a little too far, or that he was too big to carry, but the dragon smiled and nodded.

"It will be my pleasure, although it might be a bit bumpy as my wings are a bit creaky and I can't go too far as I'm not quite up to my old speed... Come back tomorrow night and we'll see what we can manage."

The new friends parted, each thrilled with their new friendship. Angus ran home to the cottage and just made it into bed when his parents came home from the pictures. By the sounds of it they had come home via the local pub as well. Dad was being noisily quiet by bumping into things and speaking in his loud whisper. Mum was telling him not to make too much noise but giggling while she did so.

"Are you sleeping love?" she asked quietly as she popped her head in the door.

He pretended to be half asleep and half raising his head he replied,

"Uurgh... Mum. You're back. Oka..."

For good effect he didn't finish the last word and flopped his head sleepily back into the pillow. He was rewarded with a quiet chuckle and she closed the door quietly before dragging his Dad off to bed. Lying in the dark Angus could not think about anything else but Pyrra and what she had told him. Eventually he dropped off to sleep and dreamt about flying on a dragon's back.

The following morning Angus could not resist the opportunity of passing the dragon in the High Street and went straightaway to speak to his new friend. Being Sunday the streets and the square still bore the scars or the market that had taken place the day before. Rubbish lay on the ground where people, too lazy to put it in the bins, had dropped it. Some of the stallholders still had the frames to take down and various piles of empty boxes grew like small cardboard mountains from the cobbles in the square.

Despite his usual advances he was disappointed to find the dragon stayed solemn and silent, not acknowledging his presence at all. No amount of harrumphing or entreating would crack that painted stare. Perhaps he had imagined the whole episode, but wait! His pocket was empty in his clean trousers and he turned on his heel and fled back to the cottage, fearing the worst. The precious Dragonore may have been dissolved by Kleanware's very popular non-biological washing powder or may at this very moment be rattling round in the washing machine on its spin cycle! Fortunately his jeans were where he had left them; crumpled in a heap on his bedroom floor. 'Phew!' He resolved to take greater care of his precious rock and intended to return to see Pyrra that night, his last before going home.

The night could not come quick enough for Angus; the hours seemed to drag and his parents stayed in the pub for what seemed like ages. He had to wait until they had gone to bed and were snoring loudly before he got dressed and opened his bedroom door as silently as he could. Making sure that he had the rock this time he crept out of the cottage and ran down the road. Pyrra seemed to be twinkling in the moonlight, inviting him to come nearer and the contents of his pocket glowed as he apprehensively moved towards the sweetshop.

He was feeling a bit sick with nerves. It was one thing to dream about flying through the sky on a dragon's back, but to actually do it was another matter!

Angus approached the plinth, secure in the knowledge that this time the Dragonore was safe in his pocket. The dragon stood solemn and still as before, it seemed his greeting fell on deaf ears. He reached out and as he touched the painted nose, suddenly the dragon blinked and acknowledged him.

"Sorry Angus, I was asleep. So you've decided to take me up on that flight then?"

He could only nod in reply.

There was no going back now! The moment he couldn't wait for had finally come and he was terrified! Pyrra invited Angus to climb upon her green scaly back. His legs turned to jelly and he felt quite sick with apprehension. With a quick glance up and down the empty High Street, Pyrra told Angus,

"Close your eyes and hold on tight."

He wiped his sweaty palms on his trousers, took a deep breath and did as he was bid, but opened his eyes again in disbelief, for he could feel the hard shell of her painted body soften and mould around his fingers – the shell was turning into warm scales! He could hardly believe what was happening!

"Whoa…" Now he was being thrown this way and that as the dragon grew and grew until she was almost the size of a minibus! He clung on with all his might and shifted his position on her back to make his seat more secure. Pyrra deftly unfurled her great green wings and started beating them faster and faster, building up power like a steam train.

Swiftly and silently upwards, boy and dragon ascended into the night sky.

"Woohoo! Wicked!" he cried.

Angus was more excited than he had ever been in his life, he could not believe this was happening to him. It was just like in the story. Below them some late night revellers were coming out from the pub and he was worried that their flight would be discovered! What if someone saw them and phoned the police! How would he explain this to his parents? Hopefully the jostling crowd, spilling out onto the pavement below had had a drink and they wouldn't believe what they were seeing anyway!

The pair rose higher and higher above the rooftops and Angus had to bite his lip until it bled to stop himself shouting too much in case anyone heard him.

"Don't worry, you are quite invisible," reassured Pyrra as she glanced back over her shoulder at her anxious young rider.

"No-one can see you or hear you if you are riding on a dragon's back," she explained further.

"Not unless they have Dragonore or if I want them to. If you look down there where we have come from, you will see that I have left the shell behind. So no-one will even know that I am gone." Angus followed her gaze and could make out the lifeless dragon ride below them.

"Look, I'll demonstrate, hold on tight and watch this…" and she swooped down along the High Street, almost knocking the hat off the head of a man who had just come out of the fish and chip shop. Angus ducked and gripped harder with his already white knuckles, sure that they were about to be discovered, but no-one batted an eyelid. A great green scaly dragon being ridden by a boy must be an every day occurrence in Piggleston! Either that or they truly were invisible!

"Wow!"

"Invisibility is an ancient power that we dragons still maintain" Pyrra smiled. They flew higher and higher.

"Hey, there's the railway line!" pointed Angus enjoying the perspective of the town from the air now he'd found his balance. This was truly awesome and much better than he could ever have imagined.

After a little while the dragon faltered and the rhythmic

 beating of her wings slowed ever so slightly.

"I'm tiring now" she sighed regrettably. "We must return to the plinth. I have not used my wings for many years and they are still a bit stiff."

She gathered all her strength for the descent and Angus clung on tightly to her neck. She glided swiftly but gently back to the ground and landed once more on her plinth and Angus gratefully slid off her great green back onto the pavement. He was totally buzzing but still felt a little bit sick having had quite enough excitement for one night. Angus had to pinch himself to make sure he wasn't dreaming; had he truly ridden on a dragon? No-one would ever believe him, and anyway who would he tell? His parents were not in the slightest bit interested and always too wrapped up in the world of Kleanware to listen to their son's 'childish prating'.

Meanwhile Pyrra settled herself comfortably once more on her plinth, having already morphed back down to her disguised size. She folded her green wings around her resting body; the scales turning once more to metal. Angus thanked her and hurtled home as fast as he could, his heart was thumping loudly in his chest! That was the most exciting ride he'd ever been on in his life and much cooler than any roller coaster!

Lying in bed and reliving the incredible flight he thought there was someone he could tell about his adventure after all; Miss Puttick the librarian, as she seemed to be a believer in dragons. Angus considered that part of the oath of the Secret Society of Dragon Protectors was secrecy, but if Miss Puttick did believe then she was potentially an ally and he needed a grown-up on his side to help him. He had decided from the first moment he spoke with Pyrra that he would do all he could to uphold the ancient Society's values. He would somehow become a modern day dragon protector and with Pyrra and Miss Puttick's help he would track down as many hibernating dragons as he could!

Chapter 4

'Blue Dragon Fire'

On his last morning in Piggleston, Angus got up very early and ran to the High Street. He squeezed as far between the shop window and the dragon ride as he could and sat down on the pavement. Hidden from view to all but the dragon, he could feel the glowing Dragonore in the pocket of his jeans. Pyrra blinked and listened to him as he eagerly asked her question after question. He needed a few answers to help him with his quest.

"These other dragons, you said there were 'not many of us left now'. Do you know what became of them? Have you any idea where they might be hibernating?" Pyrra kept perfectly still, thought for a moment and then answered him in her soft creaky tones.

"One of the problems with our hibernation is that when we do awaken it takes a while to sort out our memories. They're all still intact, but it just takes a bit of time to put them in order. Well, once there were many of us... but among my special friends were Godroi, Argent, Rhys and Cyru," she reminisced.

"Now Godroi, or Godroi the Golden if I give him his full title, he was the one the knight George was supposed to have slain but actually the knight made a pact with him and Godroi went off to live in a cave somewhere... Then there was Argent the Silver, dear Argent loved music very much and was never far from a place he could hear it." Pyrra paused for a bit and had a hint of a dreamy look on her face but it was hard to tell as the features of the shell did not change as a normal face would.

"What about the others?" Angus asked quietly. Blinking, Pyrra replied,

"Oh yes! The others, now where was I?" she seemed to collect her thoughts for a moment and then continued. "Rhys the Red started hiding on the Welsh flag but was happiest amongst flowers, so she moved on to a garden somewhere.

That leaves Cyru the Blue. He loved sport and noisy crowds and was the most trusting and foolish of all my friends. I have no idea where he might be. If they are still in hibernation they may have forgotten how to re-awaken or just lost the will to do so. They would have probably chosen suitable places to hide and used shells much as I did. Now that I can remember them, it would be marvellous to meet up again."

"One last question before I go?" added Angus. "This address in the pamphlet, a house called Long Reach in

Lower Dinton? Do you remember if that is the headquarters of the SSDP?"

"Ah. Let me think now…….. No, it was definitely not a house. I can't remember what it was exactly. Somewhere we dragons liked to visit, bigger than a house… but I do recall Finian Tek though." Angus' attention was focused on her scaly face now. "He used to visit me from time to time. That was many years ago though and I have not seen him in a long time."

Angus, slightly disappointed, wondered if the SSDP pamphlet or 'Dragonalia' might hold any more clues that he had missed and he left a thoughtful looking Pyrra; no doubt reviving old memories rekindled by the questions that he had asked. She seemed quite at home surrounded by ice-cream wielding infants. He left, promising to return soon.

As Angus walked, he anguished long and hard over how he could best help his dragon friend. Was there some way of finding the lost dragons? If he were able to reawaken them with the help of the knowledge of the SSDP, where could they go to live peacefully? He needed to re-read the pamphlet. When he arrived back at the cottage his Mum and Dad were almost ready to go but of course his Dad still had the mobile phone glued to his ear…

"So that's two bottles of Kleanware's super stain remover..." Naturally Angus just got on with packing and loading the van. Dad finished his call and looking quizzical asked,

"Where have you been son? Not back to that sweet shop again?"

"Yeah, I just like it there. What of it?" Angus replied half thinking that his Dad might have seen him talking to the dragon.

"Well if I had thought you were that easily pleased I would just have bought you a massive bag of sweets and then we could have stayed at home," his Dad joked. Angus just gave a half hearted laugh, typical of his Dad to pretend this sales weekend was for Angus' benefit!

Angus was the first one through the front door of the house and he sifted through the Kleanware envelopes on the mat. Mr Tek had not answered yet and Angus was rather disappointed to find no letter the next morning either. A little later he leaned his bike against the familiar red brick wall of the library and entered to breathe in the musty smell of books.

The librarian was delighted to see him; she had missed his company and his dragon filled conversations.

"Miss Puttick, can I tell you a secret?" Angus eagerly asked, "But first I need to know if you believe in dragons." Miss Puttick was a little sceptical about the whole dragon issue and although bemused she could not resist the boy's innocent enthusiasm, so she solemnly declared that she did believe. Angus went on to tell her all that had happened during his stay in Piggleston. When he had finished, Miss Puttick let out a low whistle through her teeth and pushed her half-spectacles back onto her nose.

"Well, now what are you going to do?" she peered closely at the boy, half fearing his answer.

"I need your help" Angus replied, "I think we must start looking for clues to the locations of the lost dragons. If only I could find the headquarters of the SSDP but the pamphlet doesn't mention it. Finian Tek runs the SSDP but I have no idea where he might be."

"I can see your problem," she replied. "Didn't this dragon, what was it called?"

"She... Pyrra!" corrected Angus.

"Yes...Pyrra. Didn't she give you any clues?"

"A few, but she couldn't remember the location of the headquarters. I have re-read the pamphlet and apart from the address that I sent the letter to, I can't find anything... I guess it's a secret, but I was sure Finian Tek would leave some sort of clue if he wanted to be found."

Miss Puttick seemed to ponder this thought for a minute and then, of course, it had been right in front of her all the time.

"Wait a minute!" she exclaimed, pushing her useful matchbox across her desk to an incredulous Angus. "This might be the clue you are looking for. The man who gave me the book left this as well. Remember... this held the Dragonore!" she said triumphantly.

Angus studied the matchbox and the small picture on it.

"Calmor Castle" he read out loud, "never heard of it."

"Well I think we can find that," replied Miss Puttick. After hours of extensive searching in the libraries reference books; then on the Internet, they were disappointed to find no information about Calmor Castle.

"That is strange," said a puzzled Miss Puttick. "You would think there would be some sort of literature on a castle like that."

Angus dejectedly looked again at the medieval castle. It was on what looked to be an island, surrounded by brilliant blue flowers, the likes of which he had never seen before. Then he remembered that he had seen them somewhere. He had read about them, but where?

Suddenly it came to him! He reached for 'Dragonalia' on the shelf and flicked through the pages. He found a reference to a very rare plant species.

"Miss Puttick, look at this. I'm sure this is a clue," he said as he walked over to where she sat at the computer. "According to this, dragons are drawn to this plant because of its unusual aniseed scent. It doesn't say where it grows but it is almost extinct; and look, it's the flower pictured on the matchbox!"

"CAERULEUS DRACONIS IGNIS," she read out loud.

"Which literally translates as Blue Dragon Fire," finished Angus.

"Well done Angus!" she exclaimed, raising her voice more than was usual in the library.

Surely all they had to do was find the native habitat of this rare plant and hopefully that would lead them to the location of Calmor Castle and the headquarters of the SSDP. Angus felt certain that there they would find some clues as to where the other dragons were hibernating. Miss Puttick sighed thoughtfully, fiddled with her glasses for a moment and then jumped up with alarming agility.

"Well of course!" She rushed over to the Botanical Section and started running her expert fingers along the spines of the many books on world plant species.

"Ah ha!" she said, pulling out a weighty leather tome with some Latin inscription on the front. She leafed through the pages in an efficient librarian manner and triumphantly thrust the book on the table, with her finger on the relevant listing.

"Here it is! CAERULEUS DRACONIS IGNIS more commonly known as Blue Dragon Fire has distinctive blue flowers and an overwhelming aniseed scent. Also thought to contain healing properties," she finished triumphantly.

"Now that explains why Pyrra was rather partial to cough candy," Angus mused, "What does it say about its natural habitat?"

"A hardy plant found only on rocky areas. Now very rare and can only be seen on The Maidens," announced Miss Puttick.

Leaving Angus looking confused, she strode to the other end of the reference section to find an atlas.

"Maidens…. Maidens…well, well, that's something! I've never heard of them but they are apparently a group of small islands located just off the Irish Coast."

"At least they're in the British Isles!" laughed Angus, who was perhaps a little disappointed that his quest wasn't going to take him to a destination further afield.

"And look at that!" he shouted, pointing to the open 'Atlas of The British Isles', "Those islands which make up The Maidens, they almost look dragon shaped!"

With Miss Puttick holding her head to one side and squinting at the page Angus' mind then turned to more practical matters. At least it would be quite feasible to visit The Maidens accompanied by Miss Puttick as a sort of field trip. Though getting there would be a problem. Maybe once Pyrra had practised flying a bit more she could take them. It didn't look to be too far; at least not as the dragon flew. They were somewhere just off the coast of Ireland but first he had to persuade Miss Puttick to come to Piggleston with him to meet Pyrra.

"Miss Puttick do you have a bike?"
As he had been thinking, the librarian was watching him with interest. She could guess what had been going through his mind and was wondering how she could persuade him not to go off gallivanting on some adventure.

"Why would I need a bike?" she replied with a nervous laugh.

"Well, I was hoping you would like to come with me to meet Pyrra and... you know... tell her what we've learned."

"Me? Go with you?" the librarian was astonished that he would ask her to meet his dragon. She was not quite sure whether to encourage him in this foolish adventure or not but she was equally excited by the boy's infectious enthusiasm.

"I can't remember the last time I went on an outing!"

"Oh please," he pleaded, "I don't want to have to go on my own and I would love to introduce you to Pyrra. It's the only way you will believe me."
She looked at his imploring eyes and quite against her better judgement she sighed,

"It will have to be on Sunday when the library is closed."

"Brilliant Miss P! You're the best!" laughed Angus. "You'd better come home with me after closing today so I can explain to my parents."

"What are you going to tell them?" she enquired.

"Oh I'll think of something, they're too busy to take to much notice and they've known you for years... maybe I'll tell them you're helping me with a school project or something."

Angus was right. His parents were quite relieved to hand over their son to a responsible adult's care for a day's bike ride. It was, after all, one thing less for them to worry about so wrapped up as they were with their orders and deliveries.

"Yes that will be lovely Miss Puttick but I hope Angus will behave himself and not be too much trouble," said Angus' Mum as she shepherded Miss Puttick to the front door.

"Angus is a fantastic boy and always well behaved when he comes to the library, so I think he will be fine."

"That's lovely," she said again. "Thank you for coming." After she closed the door she said more to herself than Angus;

"Right, now I must get on with those orders." She was halfway down the hall when she suddenly turned to Angus again.

"Oh someone was here looking for you, Angus. Some Mr...Tek"

"What did he say Mum?" enquired the lad eagerly.

"Not quite sure what he wanted. He didn't say anything other than that you had written to him, wouldn't leave a number or anything."

"Didn't he leave any message at all?" implored Angus.

"He said he would call back again but didn't say when." Although disappointed to have missed him, Angus was secretly thrilled! Finian Tek had not only replied but had come to see him. The author of 'Dragonalia' and the head of the SSDP had been here!

"He was a little strange looking… What did you write to him about?"

"Oh… er… just the project thing I am working on."

"Okay dear. I could do with some help. It's August now and all the new orders have to go out in the next couple of days. You know what to do to get them ready and you might as well help to deliver as well."

"Yeah okay" replied Angus with a total lack of enthusiasm. Shame Finian Tek didn't leave a telephone number or something.

After four days of trudging up and down endless streets delivering Kleanware products and collecting money, Angus was glad to wake up on Sunday morning knowing that he was going to see Pyrra again. He had only seen Miss Puttick briefly once or twice that week, and only then to make sure she didn't back out at the last minute. He was waiting at the library as agreed with his favourite backpack and had brought something to eat and drink, including some sweets for Pyrra. He was just beginning to wonder if the librarian had decided not to come when he heard a squeaking noise. Angus was greatly amused and somewhat embarrassed by the appearance of Miss Puttick on a boneshaker of a bike that looked like it had come out of a museum. It was black and very upright with a crossbar. She looked comical, perched on the high saddle in her tweed suit and sensible brogues with an old beanie hat on her head. He was pleased that they wouldn't be going far and hopefully no-one would see them! Thankfully there were no hills between Kynton and Piggleston as she certainly did not have gears on her ancient bike.

"Hi Miss P!" he called to her as she pulled up.

"Hello Angus" she replied breathlessly, wobbling along the kerb. Angus could tell this was going to be a slow ride to Piggleston.

"Can I fix that for you?" He pulled some oil from his backpack and lubricated the wheels and chain of her bike. They set off and having cured the squeaking of her ancient bike they had a very uneventful ride to Piggleston. It wasn't long before the librarian found herself standing outside Mrs James's sweetshop in the middle of the High Street, face to face with the dragon ride.

It was the middle of the morning by the time they got there and Pyrra was busy giving children rides. Angus was keen to introduce the two ladies and it amused him that he used to think of Miss Puttick as a bit of a dragon before he got to know her properly. He realised they should wait until a quieter time so they would remain unobserved. Whatever would people think if a boy and a grown woman were to be seen talking to a children's ride? They strolled along the High Street for a bit, peering in shop windows and Miss Puttick bought tea and scones in the Silver Kettle cafe. It was a nice treat and Angus quietly told her again what Pyrra had said about the other dragons.

They returned to the sweet shop when all the shopkeepers were drawing down the blinds and finishing up for Sunday lunch. Angus was pleased to find the High Street had quickly emptied and as usual he touched the Dragonore in his pocket to check he still had it. At first nothing happened and Miss Puttick was preparing herself to console the lad but then Pyrra blinked and smiled at her young friend and looked nervously at Miss Puttick who was doing an excellent goldfish impression. She hadn't really believed the boy and just went along with his fanciful tale but she was swiftly changing her mind.

"Pyrra may I introduce Miss Puttick, Miss Puttick, this is Pyrra."

Miss Puttick gasped and then tried to compose herself.

"I... It's not every day that Aurora Puttick gets to converse with a dragon" she stammered. She took a step nearer and opened the clasp of her old-fashioned handbag.

"How do you do?" said Miss Puttick politely, "I've brought you something, Madam," she said, and reaching in the bag, she pulled out a piece of dried Blue Dragon Fire carefully wrapped in a lace hanky.

"Where on earth did you get that from?" Angus whispered incredulously.

"I found it pressed in the back of the pamphlet before I gave it to you" she replied.

Angus thought he saw a tear in Pyrra's eye. She was overwhelmed by the gift. He told her about their discoveries and that they knew of the location of Calmor Castle. "I think it might be the headquarters of the SSDP and hopefully we might find some more information about your friends."

"So you are planning to go to this Calmor Castle then?" she asked, still savouring the delicious aniseed scent of the little blue flower.

"It would be great if we could go, and you would be able to find those flowers fresh and not dried," Angus fished.

"So you want me to go with you?"

"Well I was hoping you would be able to fly there. I know you are still a bit rusty but it would be so much easier to go with you," pleaded Angus ignoring Miss Puttick's shocked look.

"Well I am not so rusty now. I have been practicing since our last flight."

"Wow that's great!" shouted Angus. "So you'll do it then?"

"Oh absolutely, I think it's time that this old dragon got some real exercise."

Miss Puttick had been listening to this exchange in disbelief. She had to pinch herself a couple of times to make sure she was awake. Yet there she was standing talking to a small dragon in the middle of Piggleston High Street outside the sweet shop!

"Pyrra is there any chance you might take Miss Puttick for a ride?" she heard Angus ask. "Just a short trip but I'd love her to experience a dragon flight like I did!"

"Oh no, that's fine, I'll just stay right here on the pavement and watch if you don't mind," she heard herself saying.

"It will be my pleasure, Angus" replied Pyrra beckoning the flustered librarian to hop on her back.

"Nooo... no, I couldn't possibly... I get air sick... I don't have the proper clothing... I... I..." she found herself stammering and stuttering but Angus seemed to be enjoying her discomfort and wasn't taking no for an answer. Oh well, there was only one thing for it, she'd have to grit her teeth and do the British thing, stiff upper lip and all that… surely it wouldn't be that bad. It was after all only a very small dragon… But of course Miss Puttick didn't know that Pyrra was about to morph into the size of a minibus! Angus held her handbag and the terrified librarian hitched up her tweed skirt and inelegantly clambered on to the dragon's back. Angus could barely contain his laughter as he looked at Miss Puttick, a grown woman, sitting on top of a kiddies ride.

"Hold tight," shouted Pyrra and Angus in unison as Pyrra started to twitch violently, throwing the startled passenger from side to side, much in the same way as a rider on a camel when it gets up off its knees. Angus had a fit of the giggles as Miss Puttick, normally so neat and orderly, was being flung violently around like a rodeo rider. Her hair, always tidy in a bun, was straggling around her face and her half glasses seemed in danger of sliding off her nose at any minute.

"Hold tight Miss Puttick," he shouted as he jumped on behind her wrapping his arms around her waist to hold them both steady. Pyrra didn't really have a mean bone in her scaly body even though she was amused by Angus' sense of boyish mischief. However she didn't want to upset the librarian and she began to lift off the ground as gently as she could. Pyrra pushed higher into the air and completed a gentle circuit of the town square just above the tree line, despite Angus' urging to go further and higher. Miss Puttick eventually settled into the rhythm of the great beating wings and once she opened her eyes properly and relaxed her throttle-like grip a little, she found she was actually enjoying the experience.

"I think that will do for today" said the dragon who was being considerate and started a gentle gliding descent which greatly relieved Miss Puttick.

Safely back on her plinth once more, Pyrra discharged her passengers and looked at Angus who was now leaning heavily against the window of the sweetshop convulsed with laughter. She reminded him,

"Now Angus you were not so fearless during your first flight if you remember."

He finally managed to pull himself together.

"I'm sorry Miss Puttick; it's just that you looked so funny when Pyrra was changing. I really did think you were going to end up on the pavement!"

Miss Puttick dusted herself down and straightened her skirt, tucking the stray bits of hair back in her bun.

"Yes well, that's quite enough adventure for one day… thank you Pyrra… a pleasure to meet you… come along Angus it's time to go."

Her authoritative tone belied the fact that her pulse was racing and she felt like a teenager again. She cycled all the way home to Kynton with the energy of a youngster free wheeling the last stretch. The dragon ride had really got her adrenalin rushing. When they got back to the library Angus said goodbye and told her he would be round tomorrow to discuss their plans for the journey to Calmor. She really was not looking forward to any long trip but she didn't want to tell him that. What she really wanted right at that minute was to relax with a nice cup of Earl Grey and put her feet up.

Chapter 5

'Flight to Calmor'

The next morning found Angus at the library just after opening time as he wanted to avoid being asked to do any more Kleanware work. Miss Puttick was already filing some returned books she had not completed on the Saturday and she jumped when Angus called her name.

"Oh Angus, you gave me such a fright."

"Sorry, I thought you heard me come in."

"To be honest Angus I have not been myself this morning. I keep filing books in the wrong place."
She walked over to her desk and put down the books she still had in her hands. Angus followed her and noticed that she was definitely not her usual cool and calm self. She seemed to be on edge and a bit distracted.

"What's wrong Miss Puttick?" he enquired.

"Well…. It's…Oh it's nothing. I'm just being silly."

"No really, what's the matter? Are you having second thoughts about the trip?"

"Now that you mention it, yes I am. I was convinced that this was all in your head Angus but now I have seen Pyrra for myself..... Well I don't know what to think."

Angus could see where this was going and was prepared for it. Mum and Dad did this when they didn't want to do something that Angus wanted to do. He decided to play his trump card.

"If you don't want to go then I understand. It is a bit scary flying with dragons and going to strange places and I can go by myself if you want."

Judging by the look on Miss Puttick's face it had worked.

"Not at all Angus, I am just concerned for your safety and about what your parents will think. I mean we will have to be away for a couple of days at least. It will take Pyrra hours to fly such a distance."

Miss Puttick was right. Angus had only seen Pyrra fly twice but she had not flown that fast, or very far.

"Maybe she can fly faster than we saw last night. I can go and ask her."

"I think that would be best Angus, as otherwise we will have to come up with a fantastic excuse for your parents and I am not sure they will believe that it's part of some school project."

Angus decided he would go to Pyrra the very next day straight after breakfast.

By nine o'clock the next morning he was in the High Street and pleased to see that nobody was in sight. He leant his bike against the wall and walked up to Pyrra. He could still not take it in that she was a real dragon and was startled into realising he had been staring when Pyrra asked,

"Well, have I got bird pooh on my head or something?"

"No Pyrra, sorry I was just sort of day dreaming," replied Angus embarrassed.

"I actually need to discuss something really important with you… you know, about the trip."

"Ah. I though you might be asking about that," Pyrra smiled.

"Well it's the distance and the time. How long will it take you to fly there?"

"Well it depends on what you mean by time Angus. I can fly pretty fast and I can seem to fly faster but I assure you we will be there and back again in less than a day," she replied, amused at the look on his face.

"Really… can you fly that fast?" gasped Angus, his face giving away his incredulity.

Feeling satisfied that the trip would be a lot shorter than he had at first thought, though not understanding how, he sped back to the library to tell Miss Puttick the good news.

After explaining the conversation to her she still looked upset but refused to let on what was bothering her.

"So we can go now without making up any elaborate stories" he finished.

"Well okay I suppose. I wonder how fast she can actually travel. It must be extremely fast to do that distance in such a short time. How will we stay on her back?" she queried.

Angus didn't know but he was sure that Pyrra would not let them come to any harm and assured Miss Puttick of the same.

"What will you do about the library, Miss Puttick?"

"Have you not noticed the sign on the door, Angus? The library is closed for the next two weeks," she said smiling at him. "Even Librarians get holidays you know."

He said goodbye to her but, before leaving, he made sure that they would meet at the library in two day's time and that she was still going to Calmor.

A couple of days later the dragon took to the skies unseen, with two intrepid, if somewhat anxious, passengers in pursuit of… of what exactly? They didn't really know what they expected to find, but they hoped there would be some clues at Calmor Castle as to the whereabouts of Finian Tek and the rest of the Secret Society of Dragon Protectors. Angus hoped it was, as it appeared to be, the headquarters of the SSDP. He had shown Pyrra the map so that she knew roughly where to go and they set off at a reasonable speed. Angus could see the fields and woods passing below as they climbed higher and higher into the sky. He wondered how high they would go and just as he thought this Pyrra shouted back,

"I need to climb to the cloud base if I am to go faster. Once I speed things up I will no longer be invisible."

Angus was surprised at this news and was dying to ask why but since Pyrra was beating her wings harder to get higher, he had to concentrate more on holding on. At last her wings began to beat with less ferocity as they started to enter the clouds and the riders relaxed a little bit as it didn't seem as bad flying up there. They could not see the ground for a start, which was a couple of thousand feet below and Pyrra's wings made the cloud swirl around them as they settled into an easy rhythm. Miss Puttick found her voice and managed to croak a barely audible "Wonderful!"

"Aren't you worried about your parents missing you when you keep disappearing for your bike rides?" asked Pyrra. Miss Puttick who knew the answer to this did not say anything. She did not approve of the lack of time they spent with Angus.

"Not really," replied Angus. "They're too wrapped up in Kleanware to notice what I do during the daytime."

"Well," piped up Pyrra, "we won't actually disappear for as long as you may think; I already told you we dragons can slow down time for ourselves, just as we do when we hibernate." Not waiting for a reply she continued, "But we can also speed it up if the need arises."

"What do you mean speed it up?" shouted Angus.

"Just that" replied Pyrra. "When we hibernate we slow down so the world speeds by faster. That way we don't age as much. However when we are flying a great distance we can speed up the time for ourselves and the outside world seems to slow down."

"Wow!" was the only thing Angus could say at this point. He now wished they were not in the clouds so that he could see what happened below when everything became slower.

"It's one of our special powers. Therefore you will not really be missed by your parents, even if they are aware you are not there. To them you will only have been away for a matter of hours and not days"

Angus thought about this.

"So really it's like in the films when they talk about filming in 'bullet time'. Except that this is dragon time!"

"I don't know about bullet time but I do like the sound of dragon time Angus. I think that's a good name for it... dragon time..., yes I like that," Pyrra mused.

"So what happens now?" asked Miss Puttick.

"Well although we have magical powers they are not limitless so I will not be able to stay invisible whilst in..." she chuckled, "what did you call it? Dragon time... that is excellent."

Angus was watching the clouds and he noticed that they were still swirling but now they were doing so very slowly, as if in a slow motion replay.

"You're doing it now aren't you? We're in dragon time!" he shouted excitedly.

"Yes we are Angus, well noticed! We are no longer invisible and that is the reason I have flown into the clouds. We should be quite hidden if we stay up here and no-one will be looking for a dragon flying in the sky and anyway we are moving too fast to really be noticed."

"I didn't feel a thing" cried a much relieved, Miss Puttick. At which both Pyrra and Angus started to laugh.

Their flight towards The Maidens seemed uneventful and smooth and flying conditions were perfect. They had been flying for a couple of hours and Angus only really saw the landscape once or twice through the thinning cloud cover. It looked at one point as if they were flying over some peaks but he could only guess that it was maybe the Welsh mountains below. Miss Puttick was just nodding off when Pyrra turned her head slightly.

"By my reckoning we are not far from the coast of Galloway. I think we are still too far away to see The Maidens but you might see the Irish coast."

At these words Miss Puttick sat more upright as she had clearly heard what Pyrra had said. Both riders peered eagerly down through the clouds trying to find any feature that they could recognise.

"Hold on and I will fly a little lower to let you see more and I can get my bearings. It should be safe enough, but to be sure I have reverted back to invisibility" Pyrra shouted.

They had started to clear the lower clouds when suddenly a large winged creature flew out of the clouds and straight at them. Angus only had a split second to realise it was a glider! Pyrra pulled up sharply to avoid a head on collision. Of course the invisible dragon and her passengers were unseen by the glider pilot, who had no idea that a dragon was in his flight path. Pyrra's erratic manoeuvre had thankfully managed to avert certain disaster. She had just levelled back out when she heard Miss Puttick screaming. That was when Pyrra realised the frantic librarian was telling her that Angus had fallen from the dragon's back when she took evasive action.

"Hold on tight" she shouted and went immediately into a steep spiralling dive.

Angus was in freefall and had at first screamed his head off. He stopped doing this when, after what seemed like forever, nothing happened except for the wind rushing past his face. He looked at the ground which still seemed so far away and part of his brain told him he should scream again, which he did. He quickly realised that screaming was no use so he stopped, praying that Pyrra would be able to catch him soon. He was now hurtling down towards the sea and the coastline at an alarming rate. The streamlined dragon was almost dart like with her wings folded back along her body to garner as much speed as she possibly could. Angus was beginning to see a lot of details in the upcoming ground and knew now that he was only a few hundred feet from certain death. With calculated ease Pyrra made a very tricky manoeuvre. Spreading her wings wide at just the right moment, she was able to pluck

Angus out of the air and catch him gently in her fore claws. Miss Puttick who could hardly breathe and could not see because her eyes were streaming with water, screamed.

"Have you got him?"

"Yes… I've got him and think we should go down to the ground and make sure everyone is alright."

"Yes I think that would be best," Miss Puttick stammered.

Luckily the glider pilot had not glanced behind him or he may have seen a boy falling like a stone from the sky, as once he had left the safety of the dragon's back he was quite visible to anyone who cared to look his way. As Pyrra gently glided down the last few hundred or so feet to the ground, Angus, who was not quite recovered, noticed something he had not had an opportunity to see before. Pyrra's chest and what was on it. The slightly shaken dragon and her companions touched down in a grassy field not far from the coastline. Miss Puttick scrabbled off the dragon and onto the grass where she promptly lay down as if to touch as much of it as she could. Pyrra was quite upset by the incident.

"I'm so sorry…I just don't know where it came from, that great silent bird! I just didn't see it coming!"

Angus was still a bit shaken and waved his hand to show he was fine.

"It's okay Pyrra it was a glider. A type of aircraft that doesn't have an engine," he explained.
Pyrra had never seen one of those before. As they got their breath back Angus looked again at Pyrra's chest. She saw him staring.

"Well you did say you had read we liked to hoard precious gems and use them as protection. Now you can see it is true."

Angus was indeed staring at Pyrra's underside which boasted a vast array of every kind of gemstone that you could imagine. However he was not interested in the diamonds and rubies.

"I can see the rest of them Pyrra, but the one that caught my eye is the large one in the middle."

As he said this he was pulling at a leather shoelace tied around his neck. When it came out from under his sweatshirt it had a small pouch on the end. Miss Puttick stood up and moved to Angus' side, clearly curious as to what was going on. She gasped when she saw the sparkling array of stones on the dragon's soft underside.

"I keep this in here now… for safety… I really don't want to lose it" he said as he pulled his piece of Dragonore from the pouch.

"You have a piece in your chest and when I was close to you it glowed and I could feel the heat from mine." He held up his stone to Pyrra's and they both glowed brightly, only dimming slightly when Angus took it away.

"I can see that nothing escapes your notice Angus, you're a sharp boy" said Miss Puttick.

"Indeed, the Dragonore pieces are in fact connected and through them we can enhance our powers," explained Pyrra. "It also allows us to detect others with the same stone and thus we can tell if other dragons are nearby, or dragon protectors for that matter."

Miss Puttick's eyes were wide while she looked at the stone in Angus' hand, watching its magical glow. Then she realised she was staring and said,

"Well shall we finish the last part of our journey? If I am not mistaken, it is only a short flight over in that direction and it seems a shame to waste any more time."

"If you are quite recovered, Miss Puttick?" asked Pyrra.

"Yes, yes, I am fine now. I just needed to catch my breath, once you had caught poor Angus."

"I'm okay and it really wasn't that bad" replied Angus with more bravado than he felt.

A little reluctantly the two of them climbed onto the dragon's back once more for the last leg of the journey, knowing they had no choice but to continue. Pyrra had lost a little of her confidence now and the flight was a bit bumpy. It was a short journey but they were all relieved to see the little group of islands underneath them.

Suddenly Angus could see Calmor Castle, standing proudly on the top above a cliff. He could also make out a large lighthouse at the other end of the island. His attention was drawn to a small beach just below the castle and pointing at it he shouted,

"That looks a good place to land!"

Pyrra nodded and steered herself towards the beach, coming in a few feet over the sea, thankfully making a perfect landing on the sand.

The dragon was still quite upset that she had tipped poor Angus off and given Miss Puttick such a fright, and just when she thought her old flying skills were returning to their former standard. She waited for the riders to disembark before she folded her great green wings around her almost as if she were trying to hide her embarrassment. Angus noticed her concerned and fretful demeanour and so did Miss Puttick. They both tried to console her.

"Honestly Pyrra you didn't have a chance and it wasn't like I got hurt" pleaded Angus.

"Yes Pyrra, Angus is right. I mean look at him, does he look damaged in any way?"

At this Angus gave the thumbs up sign with an encouraging smile on his face.

"And that was a fantastic bit of flying you performed to catch him. I have never seen such a manoeuvre!" Miss Puttick said with as much praise as she could convincingly muster.

At that Pyrra perked up a bit and although still a little dejected, the dragon caught the familiar delicious scent of aniseed and sniffed the air quizzically. She visibly brightened.

"This must be it!" shouted Angus, the whole drama of the flight quickly forgotten, as he spied a medieval castle with its square turrets on top of the hill. The hill seemed to be an extension of the sky, for it was carpeted in Blue Dragon Fire and looked just like the picture on the matchbox. Pyrra sidled off in the direction of the scented blue floral cushions bursting out from the rocks. She told the others she would stay there and wait for them.

"Take as long as you want," she said, hoping that being amongst the Blue Dragon Fire would soon help her put the unfortunate flying incident behind her.

"COME ON, Miss Puttick we're nearly there!" Angus shouted impatiently, now quite recovered, as he raced ahead toward the castle. Miss Puttick wheezed and panted after him, pleased she had her sensible shoes on.

"Wait for me!" she gasped, following him up the hill. Approaching the castle via a very steep and craggy path, and overwhelmed with the scent of aniseed from the Blue Dragon Fire they had disturbed, Miss Puttick wondered momentarily at their wisdom. They had no idea to whom the castle belonged and what exactly were they going to say to the owner anyway? They reached the massive oak door which was firmly shut and, despite their best efforts at knocking, showed no signs of opening. Suddenly a man in working clothes appeared from a walled garden behind them.

He had with him two extremely large and ferocious looking hounds, snapping on short leashes causing both Angus and Miss Puttick to shrink back towards the door as he advanced towards them.

Chapter 6

'Murals and Flapjacks'

The stranger kept advancing and Angus thought he
was going to set the dogs on them. However just before he
got near enough for the dogs to reach them he stopped
and exclaimed.

"Jaysis, where in God's name did you come from? And
what business would you be having here then?"

He didn't look much like the owner since he had
working overalls on and a wax jacket, though you could
never be too sure. He had a rugged outdoor look about
him with an unshaven face and unkempt hair. Angus
guessed he was probably about the same age as
Miss Puttick and he had a broad Irish accent. Miss Puttick
decided to take charge and put on her best librarian voice.

"Good day to you sir, we are studying rare plants and
we believe that this is the only place where CAERULEUS
DRACONIS IGNIS grows. Would we be correct in our
assumption?"

The man mellowed a little and smiled.

"So you'd be looking for the Blue Dragon Fire then.
Well 'tis famous the world over an' like you say Missus it
will only be growing here on Calmor. Like meself it likes the

85

rocks an' the harsh Irish Sea breezes, but eh… just who would you be now?"

"Oh my apologies sir, where are my manners? This is Angus Munro and my name is Miss Puttick… Aurora Puttick," she gushed.

He was about to step forward to shake her hand when he realised that he still had hold of the dogs.

"Jaysis sorry Missus, now you two will be staying right here an' I'll put these mutts in the kennel."

He was only gone for a second or two, around the other side of the castle having dragged the reluctant dogs away. When he came back it was clear that he was pleased to have a keen audience.

"Now then where were we? My name is Dermot dear lady an' I'm the warden here on Calmor Island." They shook hands in turn. The warden invited the surprise visitors to view the rare plant more closely.

"If you will be joining me over here I can show you some of the Blue Dragon Fire up close. Ah! Would ya just smell that? There surely is nothing like the fragrance of this unique plant."

"Yes it is extremely beautiful and exactly the reason we came. Angus is studying botany and we decided to come and see it for ourselves. I do hope we are not intruding, but we had no way of contacting the island beforehand."

"So tell me Miss…"

"Aurora," Miss Puttick added.

"Aurora," he smiled. "Just how would you be getting here anyway?"

Miss Puttick was momentarily taken aback, however recovering her composure she pointed in the direction of the beach they had come from.

"Oh we came by boat and it is waiting down there for us."

Dermot stood up on his toes to try and see the boat and Angus held his breath as he looked straight at where Pyrra was lying in the Blue Dragon Fire clearly enjoying herself. Fortunately it seemed he was not a dragon protector and could not see Pyrra.

"I was hoping we could meet the owner and apologise for intruding," Miss Puttick said, surreptitiously fishing for information and at the same time trying to divert his attention from the beach.

"Oh you'd be talking about the man himself then. That'll be Rathlin Tek, he's away just now and to be sure he keeps himself rather to himself, if you know what a mean. It's as well he's not here or you wouldn't have got up the path before he set the dogs on ya. Don't like visitors that one and hates plant busybodies. When his brother died the way he did, well, he turned a bit odd." Miss Puttick made some encouraging noises and the man continued.

"In the late Master's time, that would be Finian Tek, things were very different, so they were. Now he was a true naturalist, a historian and a gentleman. Interested in rare plants and the like... Always a welcome for visitors to Calmor in them days so there was."

Angus' ears had pricked up at the mention of the last known member of the SSDP and author of the pamphlet!

"What happened to Finian?" he asked.

"Well it was a nasty business to be sure and not a nice way to go neither. Some years back he was going off on some foolish caving expedition, somewhere near the Black Sea. Madness if you ask me. Well he never did come back neither... said he was killed in a cave-in. Now Master Rathlin, his brother, well he inherited the island, the estate and the family treasure, the whole shebang you could say. This is a special place, being the last and only place growing Blue Dragon Fire known to man. Himself though, he don't look after it, no Missus, that's my job you see. They're hardy little plants but I make sure they would be coming to no harm," he finished as he lovingly stroked the leaves of the rare plant, causing the air to fill with the pungent smell of aniseed.

"They say dragons used to crave this stuff!" he said as an afterthought and laughed.

Miss Puttick turned on all her charm which was an impressive transformation for the normally stoic librarian.

"So what else do you do here?"

"Well now where would you want me to be starting? Jaysis, me Mam would cuff the side of my head if she knew I wasn't treating me guests proper like. Bless her soul. The Master won't be back 'til tomorra and I think a cup of warm tea would be just dandy. Now will your sweet self an' your lad be joining me inside then?"

He waved them through the large wooden doors, pleased to have some company for a change. As they approached the castle Angus stared up at the doors with their Celtic patterns and at the castle itself. The building looked very old and basically had a large stone front where the doors stood with windows either side. It had two impressive square turrets at either side and Angus remembered it had two more at the back. He could see at least two more floors to the castle and all the windows had small mullioned panes.

The great oak doors swung open to admit them into a small arched hallway with large grey flagstones covering the floors. The walls were panelled halfway up with plain plastered walls above and the panels were again carved with Celtic symbols similar to the big oak doors. The walls were hung with a variety of small pictures and paintings, which were themselves covered in cobwebs and grime, making them almost impossible to see. As they passed through the arch they found themselves standing in what must once have been a truly magnificent Great Hall. Angus looked around, taking in his surroundings. Everything looked rather neglected and shabby but he could see that the same Celtic theme continued throughout the castle. No doubt it had always been this way. The amusing thought occurred to Angus that his parents would have a field day with their Kleanware products. The tapestries were faded and the huge old-fashioned furniture was in desperate need of restoration as it peeped out beneath moth-eaten dust sheets. Over the fireplace hung a coat of arms that looked very familiar and carried the motto 'Magnam Bestiam Servare'. Angus couldn't remember what the Latin inscription meant although he'd seen the same crest on the Society's pamphlet. However Miss Puttick did remember.

"Serving the great beast" she whispered.

Surrounding the crest were many portraits of severe looking men, all with similarly chiselled features. Presumably these formidable gentlemen were former owners of Calmor Castle. The two most recently painted portraits stood either side of the fireplace, one with laughing eyes and a friendly face; the other more austere with almost a sneer on his thin face. Angus looked around at the rest of the Hall taking in the stairs that swept majestically up at either side of the great stone fireplace and disappeared into darkness. It was at this point he then stopped dead in his tracks. Turning his head back towards his left, on one of the long sides of the Great Hall, where the light streamed in through the mullioned windows were the much faded but still visible murals of six splendid dragons. He could not believe his eyes! The warden, Dermot, had left them on their own for a moment whilst he disappeared down a small stone staircase to the kitchen muttering about making tea. Quick as a flash, Angus pulled out a notebook from his backpack and started to make rough sketches of the dragons on the walls and he wrote a few notes to help him remember what he was seeing. Miss Puttick realised what he was doing and went down the side staircase to try to distract Dermot and give the lad a bit more time. Angus quickly realised that what he might actually be looking at was the key to the location of the lost dragons Pyrra had described.

In the first picture, a majestic golden dragon was lying at the feet of a knight, but not in a defeatist attitude like the normal depiction. They looked like friends as the knight himself did not appear to be in the usual mighty and all conquering manner. He seemed a rather more jovial man, smiling, although encased in an uncomfortable looking suit of armour. This extraordinary scene seemed to be depicted in a church window, for the surround was arch-shaped and the colours, brilliant jewel colours like you might find in stained glass. On top of the church there were two towers and a large bell with pictures and possibly writing on it. He couldn't read the inscription though.

Moving on to the second picture, this showed a splendid silver dragon who seemed to be in raptures listening to some kind of music. There were depictions of musical notes surrounding the prancing dragon. Angus jotted all this down.

"Did you say you have rare healing herbs in the kitchen garden?"

Angus could hear Miss Puttick trying to detain Dermot in the kitchen to give him enough time to finish his task. He quickly moved on to the third picture at the end of the Great Hall. This was of a stunning red dragon in a beautiful old-fashioned sort of garden next to a house with a weather vane on the top.

A mystic eastern scene followed with what looked like a pyramid in the background. This strange looking dark green dragon seemed a bit like a hieroglyphic. Angus vaguely remembered symbols like it in one of Mr Master's history lessons.

Another picture showed a grinning blue dragon, on what looked like some sort of sign on a building and the last picture was of a marvellous green dragon in full flight, soaring up into the clouds with a waving crowd of children below. Just as he closed his notebook and stuffed it in his backpack Dermot appeared at the top of the stairs carrying a tea tray with Miss Puttick following behind. She gave Angus an anxious look, undetected by the bearer of the tea tray.

"Mmmm, flapjacks – my favourite" enthused Angus, trying to convey that he had found what he wanted to Miss Puttick. He could barely conceal his excitement at their discovery. He wasn't sure what these paintings signified but he felt sure it was something relating to the SSDP and the lost dragons. Although exactly what, he could not tell. He cautiously sounded out the caretaker who was shovelling sugar into his own tea.

"Neat paintings, have you any idea what they are supposed to be?" Angus said through a mouthful of flapjack.

"Well I would not be knowing about them lad as I'm only looking after the affairs outside. All I can tell you is that they were here long before my time... Master Finian was rather partial to them though, but I've heard Himself talk about whitewashing over the whole lot. Each to their own I suppose but they would be doing no harm where they are. To be sure this place is full of dragon paintings... there's more in the turret room but no-one ever gets to go in there though... master's office."

Angus had known that there must be more dragons than what he could see on the walls and was extremely pleased to know that more paintings existed. As Miss Puttick and Dermot talked about plants he imagined himself in the same room but the walls were covered in dragon paintings and he would go out and discover a new dragon every day. Their conversation and Angus' day dream were interrupted by a cacophony of noise from the howling hounds, then a man's voice, distant but sharp, shouting a command to the dogs and telling them to be quiet. Silence followed.

"Oh Jaysis is it not Himself back a day early. Now we'll be for it. Best get you out of here as he has the other two dogs with him and to be sure he won't be holdin 'em back for no-one. Quick now, down them steps, through the kitchen, out across the lawn and through the brick archway" he said as he pushed Angus down the stairway.

Miss Puttick took charge and led the way as she'd been down those steps to the kitchen. They made for the back door, ran through the kitchen garden and out across the lawn. Tripping over timeworn paving stones they hurtled through the walled garden gateway, crashed downhill through some Blue Dragon Fire releasing the heady aniseed scent and found themselves once more on the path leading to the shore where they had started their adventure only a couple of hours earlier. They stopped to catch their breath, both winded by the exertions of running at full pelt over various surfaces and Angus had a stitch; no doubt due to too many flapjacks!

"That was a near miss!" panted Angus, not relishing the prospect of meeting the current Master of Calmor just yet.

"We need to get off this island fast!" gasped Miss Puttick.

ᴠhere would they find Pyrra?

 known to the fleeing visitors, a tall man with a
 ɔop was striding across the lawn with his fierce
 staying at his heels. He left through the walled
 ι gate as they did, but instead of descending the
 ɔ the shore, he took a different path and strode out,
 ing on top of the incline and out of sight.

 ᴍeanwhile Pyrra was contentedly snoring in a large
 ch of Blue Dragon Fire and as Miss Puttick woke her up
 e recognised the wistful and faraway look in the dragon's
 ɣe. Pyrra was dreaming of lost love and old friends which
 ʌngus was oblivious to. He was anxious to be gone before
the sharp-voiced man and those fierce dogs appeared on
the scene. They managed to convey their sense of
urgency to the sleepy dragon and had forgotten all about
their disastrous journey here in their haste to be off.
Miss Puttick shivered and turned her collar up against the
chill wind, which seemed to have sprung up from nowhere.
She took a last look at the now rather creepy looking
Calmor Castle, and fervently hoped she would never have
to see it again. She was terrified of big dogs and they don't
come much bigger than those huge hounds.

"C'mon Miss Puttick let's get going" said Angus
anxiously. Calmor looked a different place altogether now,

it seemed that the sun had turned its face away from The Maidens and even the hardy Blue Dragon Fire appeared to be shivering in the late afternoon shadows as the light was fading. Pyrra shook herself out of her reverie and bade the two climb aboard for the flight home, which would hopefully be calm and uneventful. Pyrra was still a little subdued as she took off; her pride was a bit dented from the earlier near miss with the glider.

From the top of the hill the tall man dressed in black with two of the large dogs by his side, watched through his small binoculars as the dragon and her two passengers ascended, gathered speed and departed the island. Without moving he watched them until they were no more than a mere dot in the sky. He smiled, replaced the binoculars in his pocket and accompanied by his dogs, set off back towards the castle.

Chapter 7

'Stained Glass and Gargoyles'

Settling into the rhythm of the long flight home, they had already gone into the clouds and were now in dragon time. Pyrra almost seemed to be on autopilot and Angus was anxious to talk about his findings.

"Pyrra I can't wait to tell you what I found!" he shouted, "In the castle, on the wall... lots of dragon paintings... I think they might be clues but I can't work them out!"

"My, my Angus you are quite the little detective aren't you? You had better tell me what you found out and maybe I can help you identify the dragons in the paintings," she smiled.

He reached into his backpack and pulled out his notebook, gripping it carefully so it would not fly away. He opened it up at the first page he came to and started to describe the painting of the silver dragon that he had taken the notes on. No sooner had he finished when Pyrra replied,

"That has to be Argent. Oh what a handsome beast he was! How that dragon loved to listen to music. Couldn't play a note himself of course, or sing for that matter... tone deaf... but very partial to music, particularly Widor's

Toccata belted out on a church organ if I remember correctly. He was also very light on his feet... loved to dance."

"Excellent, but do you know where he is from the picture I described?"

"Not really. It could be anywhere that has an organ... that was his favourite instrument."

Angus described the picture with the red dragon next and Pyrra seemed to think for a second or two before answering,

"Ah yes, Rhys the beautiful scarlet dragon. You know how much we dragons love Blue Dragon Fire but Rhys loved all flowers more than any of us. She was at her happiest in a garden, amongst sweet-scented flowers; surrounded by birdsong and free from the cares of the world." The dragon sighed and slowed her rhythm a little and seemed lost in a world of memories. "I don't know which garden she would have chosen though. Perhaps it will come back to me once I have had time to think about it." Angus turned the page again and described the unusual pyramid with the hieroglyph in front.

"I've no idea who that could be;" replied Pyrra, "better try the next one."

Disappointed he described the next mural and said hopefully,

"What about the blue dragon, Pyrra? Who's that?"

"Oh that's young Cyru, the most foolish of all my friends. He was very keen on human sports and therefore liked to be near to places where these events took place. He was easily led though and therefore always in trouble. Often needed rescuing by the rest of us" she sighed.

He turned the next page and told Pyrra about the children looking up at the sky and the flying dragon.

"Next one's a green one, any ideas?"

"Why don't you know Angus, that's me of course" laughed the dragon. "Going off on one of my journeys, back to my cave in the mountains I shouldn't wonder... I'd love to go back and have a look around the old place again... if only I could remember where it was... the old memory's not as sharp as it was."

"Wait I have one more!"

He flicked back the pages and came to the first painting he had seen. After describing the knight and the dragon Pyrra started to chuckle.

"Ah, dear Godroi...I always had a soft spot for him. Remember I told you about him... he really is such a clever chap. The knight in the picture is St George; he was supposed to have killed Godroi and was about to run him through with his lance when Godroi talked him round. He could charm the birds out of the trees that one and he impressed the knight so much with his wit and quick thinking that they made a pact and George actually let him go free. So you see he didn't kill him at all."

"Wow," said Angus.

"They even became best friends," continued Pyrra. "The knight was probably the first ever dragon protector, long before the Society ever came into existence. However to keep his reputation as a fearless Knight, Godroi agreed to disappear so that brave George would keep his credibility. If you remember I told you he went off to live in a cave. Now he sees himself depicted on church windows everywhere as the 'Vanquished One'. Good triumphing over evil and all that, but as you can see in this painting it's a long way from the truth. George used to visit him often… a lovely chap I seem to remember…" she tailed off deep in thought again.

"Your instincts were right then, Angus" said Miss Puttick. "Calmor Castle does indeed seem to hold the key to the lost dragons' whereabouts."

Miss Puttick had kept quiet up until that point but was keen to share her theories with Angus and Pyrra. She thought she had recognised the church from Angus' description of the wall painting. Having been too busy creating a diversion to look at it properly in the castle, she had not realised the significance of the picture until now.

"But we still don't know the locations" he said sadly.

"Well, I think I know the last one."

"REALLY?" shouted Angus.

"Yes, I think it's St George's church in Marnham. It has two towers. Well one tower and a spire to be exact. The tower has a bell in it and it certainly sounds like the same one you describe. I will go to the library tomorrow and check."

"Great! But the library is closed Miss Puttick. How can we get in?"

"Now Angus, what is the point of being the librarian and not having the privileges that go with it? Besides, I have the keys and apart from the odd council maintenance worker we will have the place to ourselves."

"Fantastic, we can all fly off that night and see if you are correct!"

"Why wait, Angus?" said Pyrra, "We can go as soon as you can get to me."

"Surely we need to do this at night when no-one will see us, don't we Pyrra?" asked Angus, surprised that Pyrra suggested a daytime flight. But he had forgotten that dragons and their riders were invisible so Pyrra reminded him of that.

"I think I will stay and do the research in the library" said Miss Puttick quickly. "I will be much more useful in that respect anyway." Keen as she was to visit St George's church with Angus and Pyrra, she wasn't quite ready for another dragon ride. She firmly declined the invitation to go with them this time but only after Pyrra assured her she would take great care of her young charge.

"What news of Finian?" the dragon suddenly asked.

"I'm sorry Pyrra, but he died" he replied sadly. Angus explained what Dermot had told them and the dragon went quiet.

"It looks like the castle was the headquarters at one time, but it's not now."

The only sound now was the rhythmic beating of her great green wings. They had talked for so long that they were not that far from home and minutes later Pyrra was dropping them off just beyond the High Street, behind some trees. She flew off and they walked round the corner to see her settling back into her hidden form. They unchained their bikes from the wall near the shop and cycled back home exhausted but certainly in Angus' case, elated.

The next day when Miss Puttick got back to the library, she looked Marnham up on the Internet and found she was correct in her recognition of the church. She showed Angus where Marnham was in the 'Atlas of the British Isles' and the enthusiastic boy was obviously anxious to get off on his quest. She told him it was the unusual bell in the tower, which gave it away; she knew a thing or two about old churches did Miss Puttick.

"There is a Saxon church with a square tower and an early English spire hidden deep in the heart of the countryside in the village of Marnham and dedicated to Saint George," she read from the listing, "However what is most unusual about this church is its great bronze bell, cast in the 17th century and given to the people of Marnham in grateful thanks by King Charles the 2nd when he and his Royalist troops hid and took refuge in the village during the long and bloody Civil War," she read on. "It is a sleepy parish and a peaceful spot, laying close to the river and approachable only by footpaths. There are many ancient gravestones there; the final resting places of countless generations of families, even some who fell on both sides during the Battle of Marnham in the Civil War."

"Cool. I can't wait to go there" replied Angus, who was not usually so keen on history but very anxious to find another dragon.

"It is a lovely place… I have not been for a long while but I remember you could not hear any traffic or indeed any noise whatsoever in that tranquil place; only the sound of trout rings bubbling to the surface of the water and the occasional swoosh of the wings of passing swans as they gently glide upstream."

Angus cycled so fast from Kynton to Piggleston that he got there in record time. He spoke to Pyrra and agreed to meet her at the trees again, that way he didn't need to get on the back of a kiddies' dragon ride in front of anyone. After all he was just a bit too big for that kind of thing and Mrs James was looking at him kind of strangely, always hanging around outside her sweet shop as he did. Once on Pyrra's back though he leaned into her and urged her to go faster.

"WOO HOO!" He screamed as they swooped through cloud after cloud zigzagging as they went. It wasn't long before they started to see a town in the distance. Angus could make out the church clearly visible amongst the other buildings.

"That must be it, Pyrra. I can see a church with a spire at one end and a tower at the other and look… there's a huge bell in the top of the tower!"

A couple of nesting pigeons flew off a high ledge, cooing and chasing each other. They probably wondered what brought the sudden gust of wind but of course they were oblivious to the invisible flying dragon and resumed their courtship on the top of a gravestone.

In St George's churchyard then, a boy and a dragon glided gently to land with a soft thud on the grass during a warm and golden August day. Angus left Pyrra under a yew tree and walked up to the church. There didn't seem to be anyone around so he turned the old-fashioned circular latch on the huge, ancient oak door and listened to it creaking open. 'Bet that door could tell some tales', he thought as he stumbled over the step, worn from the feet of many generations of worshippers. He entered the cool stone interior and breathed in the musty smell which all old churches exude; a combination of ancient hymnbooks and beeswax wood polish. Angus idly picked up a wooden paddle with a handle and read a bit about the famous Marnham bell. He peered around in the half light and saw the pulpit, the font, the altar; the rows of hard unforgiving wooden pews with their modern Mothers' Union embroidered kneelers and the old battle standards hanging in the nave. Then a brilliant light caught his eye and he was drawn towards the most stunning stained glass window he had ever seen in his life. The sunlight shone through the ancient window throwing jewels of colour on the grey stone floor. He stood in awe of the beautiful prism reflection and then moved closer to study the source. In front of him was what

appeared to be a traditional depiction of St George and a dragon which was set in an arched stained glass window. Surely he had found what he was looking for!

The dragon pictured was certainly golden and Angus wasn't quite sure how to proceed, but figured he should probably go outside because if this big golden dragon was going to morph out of the window he didn't think it would fit through the door of the tiny church. Anyway it would be better if the glass shattered outside rather than inwards!

He heaved open the heavy door again and scampered round the back of the church and found the window. It took him a minute or two to find as it was not quite so easily visible from the outside as the colours seemed quite muted. Angus felt the Dragonore glowing warmly in the pouch hung around his neck.

"Godroi, is that you?" he called to the dragon in the window, but nothing moved. He called over to Pyrra who was watching him from the shade of a yew tree through half shut eyes and amused by his excitement she added her encouragement.

"Godroi, you old rogue, don't you recognise me? It's Pyrra and this is Angus, he's a friend of mine."

Suddenly the window was filled with piercing white light and it seemed to burst into a thousand fragments. Angus was afraid he would be covered in shattered glass. Instinctively he put his hands over his head and ducked down. He didn't have thick dragon scales to protect him! He stayed like that for a few seconds and after a moment or two when nothing had happened, he lifted his head cautiously and was amazed at what he saw. Instead of brightly coloured shards everywhere, the window remained intact and a full sized resplendent golden dragon stood living and breathing right next to him! He was so in awe of this stunning creature that he didn't know whether to prostrate himself before it or bow in the very least! He stood rooted to the spot and Pyrra stepped up, sensing his bewilderment.

"Godroi, how marvellous to see you," she cooed.

"Madam" saluted Godroi, almost clicking his heels and bending forward.

"You're as handsome as ever and just as charming as I remember, you old smoothie." Angus was dumbstruck in amazement as he was seeing a new side to Pyrra. Was he imagining things or were these dragons actually flirting?

"Godroi, I would like you to meet my good friend Angus. If it weren't for him I would not be here."

"Well Sir it seems I owe you a debt of thanks. You have made my century by bringing this lovely lady to see me again."

Angus could say nothing but mumbled 'you're welcome' as he was so taken aback at the sight of the splendid golden dragon in front of him. Having been properly introduced by Pyrra, he heard Godroi's tale first hand about how he had befriended the knight George. No doubt with a few embellishments for Pyrra's benefit!

After a while the dragons' started to talk about old times and this was nowhere near as good as the tale about

St George but still quite interesting. He realised he could hear organ music and decided to take a look around. He left the two of them reminiscing about the time before the Great Hibernation and thought he would go and have a proper look inside the ancient church which must have stood on that spot since practically the time the dragons roamed around. It certainly looked 9th century, Miss Puttick had told him so about three times.

Someone must have arrived as an ancient Morris Minor was parked on the gravel at the front of the church.

As he reached the front porch Angus stopped in amazement. Glancing up at the roof he saw a dragon gargoyle perched on the gutter. It had one claw cupped against its ear as if it were straining to hear something. From within the church, the organist was busily practicing. He thundered a heavy chord with a resounding crash, and then swiftly moved to the more melodic end of the keyboard. Angus recognised the theme from the film 'Star Wars'. He wasn't paying that much attention though because as he looked up at the gargoyle it seemed to be straining to listen. Was he imagining things or had the hard stone features softened and was that the hint of a smile on those stone lips? Certainly the cupped ear seemed to have grown larger since the organ playing began!

"Pyrra come quickly! I think I've found another dragon!" Angus ran back round the side of the church to where he had left the old friends.

"I think there's a dragon on the church roof!" he spluttered.

"Ah the game is up! Just when I thought I'd keep you all to myself," sighed Godroi. "Very observant Angus, Argent is here as well. He morphed himself into a gargoyle. He loves the music you see and despite being old rivals for the affections of this dear lady we are good company for each other. It is funny how we ended up at the same church! Now let me see if I can entice him down. He will come if the organ is finished playing but I can assure you he won't budge if it hasn't."

Argent didn't take much encouraging after all when he heard his adversary and his old flame Pyrra calling him.

The silver dragon leapt deftly off the church roof and morphed as he glided down to land on the grass. He was a bit apprehensive about Angus at first but Pyrra explained about the SSDP and Angus listened patiently for a while as the three old friends caught up on the last thousand years or so!

They talked of many other dragons and how they had not heard of them for so long. Angus was particularly interested when Argent started to talk about the dragons that were not happy to stay completely hidden from humans.

"Yes I am pretty sure that the one they call Nessie is one of those attention seekers. You know… the Loch Ness Monster!" he finished dramatically.

Angus started to find the situation slightly bizarre as it seemed that Argent and Godroi were each trying to outdo the other in order to impress Pyrra. It didn't help that she was encouraging both of them and lapping up the attention from the larger male dragons!

"Dear lady I have only ever had eyes for you, heart of my hearts!" gushed Argent, who was certainly silver tongued but Godroi was having none of it.

"Really Argent what about Ancilla, that feisty little thing you saw not so long ago? I've heard you spin the same line to her!" he cried.

"That was hundreds of years ago!" protested Argent. "Haven't seen her since the Wars of the Roses!"

Pyrra turned her charms on Godroi and seemed to be fluttering her eyelashes at him! Angus wanted to reach for a bucket as he thought he would be sick any minute!

"Do you remember taking me to your cave?" murmured Godroi moving closer to Pyrra. He was clearly the favourite! Angus thought he saw Pyrra blush. Well she turned a sort of purplish shade considering her skin was green to begin with!

"I've forgotten how to get there," she sighed. "I seem to be having trouble with my memories as I was in hibernation for so long."

"I am sure I can help you remember," smiled Godroi.

Argent, not to be outdone, piped up.

"Do you remember the night we two danced under the stars?"

Angus had heard enough and left them to their stories. He wanted to return to the old church for another look around. He was surprised to find the stained glass window and the gargoyle exactly as they had appeared before the dragons awakened. So Pyrra was right about leaving their alter-shells intact when they morphed out of them!

He pottered around looking at family crests and carvings but soon Pyrra called him. He left the cool interior of the musty church and stepped once more blinking into the afternoon sunshine.

"Something you should know Angus," Pyrra called.

Angus thought it was going to be some story about how she and one of the others tried to fly to the moon or some other soppy story like that. However what she did tell him really took him by surprise.

"Godroi and Argent have told me about a man that was here looking for dragons. He had a piece of Dragonore in his hand and at first they thought it was Finian."

"You both knew Finian as well?" he asked.

"Well of course we did. He used to visit as many dragons as he could. Pyrra has told us what happened to him, such a sad end to a very noble man" said Godroi.

"Yes but if this man was not Finian who was he then?"

"We don't know Angus, but there was something very suspicious about him so we decided to stay hidden. We didn't like the look of him or trust him one bit. He had long hair that looked like a horse's tail. We weren't sure what he wanted and he went away empty-handed," finished Argent.

"A horse's tail....Oh you mean a ponytail? It was tied at the back of his head?" Angus demonstrated the hair do.

"Yes that's it," confirmed Argent. "Do you know him?"

"No I don't, but I'd like to know who he is and what he wants."

"Not to worry Angus. Rest assured that all dragons are very suspicious and mistrustful of human beings, so he won't get a response from any of us."

Angus and Pyrra bade goodbye to the golden and silver dragons and watched in fascination as they morphed back into their alter-shells. He thought he saw a tear in Pyrra's eye but she protested that she was just very happy to see her old friends again. They returned to Piggleston and arrived late in the afternoon just as the shops were closing. Mrs James was just pulling down the blind of the sweetshop as Pyrra landed unseen on the plinth. Angus came round the corner on his bike having been dropped off as before.

"Wait here a second till she goes inside," whispered Pyrra and when the coast was clear Angus said,

"Thank you for a wonderful day. I'll come back as soon as I can. I need to tell Miss Puttick about everything and hopefully she will have cracked some more of the clues."

"I am looking forward to it Angus. Goodbye."

Angus cycled slowly back home in a daze, thinking about dragons.

Chapter 8

'Sweets from a stranger'

"...And then the dragons told me that the man had a ponytail! Apart from not trusting him, they didn't seem too worried about it," finished Angus at the end of a detailed account of what had happened the day before.

Miss Puttick looked at him with a mixture of disbelief and awe.

"Well?" asked Angus, "What do you think?"

Miss Puttick closed her mouth and blinked, then eventually said,

"Well I never! I wish I had come now. It sounds like it was something not to be missed... and that marvellous old church. Did you see the bell? Three dragons together... what a splendid sight that must have been..." then shaking herself from her thoughts she added, "You are not the only one who has been busy Angus."

"Have you worked out another clue?" he asked in eager anticipation.

"Yes I have and it was not an easy task. I think I have solved the blue dragon on what looks like a sign."

"Cool, so what do you think it is then?"

"Well I believe it's a pub sign" she enthused.

The librarian was in her element; she loved working out puzzles and had already looked up all the dragon pubs in the British Isles on the Internet.

"Green dragons, red dragons, golden dragons, but luckily not many blue dragons," she said cheerily. "Look I've found this one, 'The Blue Dragon', in Marmiton, what do you think? Could this be where Cyru is hiding?"

Later that morning Angus set off once more on the short but now very familiar bike ride to Piggleston. He parked his bike outside the greengrocer's shop and walked along the High Street, wanting to discuss the next move with Pyrra. As usual he had his notebook with him in his backpack and the vital Dragonore. He patted his chest just to make sure it was still safe. He was just about at the sweetshop when he saw something very disturbing which made him stop dead in his tracks. A man in long black coat was crouching down next to Pyrra and seemed to be

talking to her. There were no children in sight so he was clearly not a parent about to give his child a ride. He was touching her nose and seemed to be talking to her, but despite Angus straining he couldn't hear what he was saying above the hum of the Saturday morning traffic. Pyrra for her part remained quite still and silent. Suddenly the man stood up and strode off. Angus noticed he had a ponytail which seemed rather odd and out of place in Piggleston High Street. He realised it must be the man that Godroi and Argent spoke of the day before. Pyrra seemed quite upset by the strange visitor and other than slipping her a cough candy Angus had to leave her to deal with a young family whose three young children were all demanding rides.

Angus returned when Pyrra was free to speak.

"Who was that man Pyrra, and what did he want?" he asked.

"I don't know but I didn't like the look of him" she replied. "He had Dragonore and he tried to offer me some sweets but they were aniseed balls. Not my favourite kind. And I remembered hearing some parents telling their children not to accept sweets from strangers. I never really knew what that meant until now. I didn't trust him one little bit and I used all my powers to stay behind my shell. There was just something I didn't like about him." The dragon seemed a bit flustered and Angus tried to console her.

"Don't worry Pyrra, you did the right thing, the same as Godroi and Argent, and ignored him."

"He wanted me to go away with him. He said he had a place where I would be safe and that only he could keep me safe, no-one else could."

"I couldn't see his face Pyrra but it was definitely the same man who visited Godroi and Argent. I just don't know how he could have known where you were."

"Well I was not worried before but I am now. Maybe he was a friend of Finian Tek, but he didn't seem genuine. It was as if he had some other reason for wanting a dragon. What do you think, Angus?"

"You could be right, but there was nobody else at Calmor Castle and I don't think that Rathlin Tek was interested. At least not according to Dermot, the warden we met."

"Perhaps someone else is looking for dragons then. Someone else we don't know about yet," replied Pyrra.

"Something else has been bothering me, Pyrra. With all that has happened recently I really didn't think about it until now. Before you met Miss Puttick I had a visitor. I thought it was Finian Tek answering my letter but after the visit to Calmor and what we found out, well of course. I know now it can't have been him." Angus' brow furrowed, "So who could it have been?" he wondered, half to himself.
Pyrra looked more concerned now, at least as far as her features could give anything away on her shell.

"What did he look like, Angus?"

"That's the problem Pyrra, I didn't see him. My Mum told me a Mr Tek came to see me and they told him I was not there. He just said he would come back."

"Where did you send that letter to, Angus?"

"Ah…I've got you… because that's where the address of the SSDP is… and since this man answered my letter you think that is a good place to start looking."

"Exactly correct Angus."

"Do you think it could be the same man?"

"I am not sure but I think we have to find out," replied Pyrra.

Angus pulled out his notes and read out the address of the house that was on the pamphlet.

"Long Reach House in Lower Dinton, Wellshire," he confirmed. "Do you know how to get there?"

"I think so but I don't know it very well" replied Pyrra. Angus knelt down, delving into his backpack and pulling out a tatty old book.

"I had a feeling this might come in handy. It's my Dad's route finder. We should be able to find the way on this. I will have a look for the location if you can meet me at the trees in a couple of minutes."

Pyrra met Angus at the trees as asked and Angus pointed to a spot on the well-thumbed map.

"That's the place… and we are here. It's only about ten miles north of here."

"Let's go then," replied Pyrra who was eager to find out who this stranger was. Angus picked up his backpack, jumped up onto Pyrra's back and they set off into the sky.

Pyrra and Angus made the short flight to Lower Dinton in no time at all. In fact even without dragon time it would still not have taken Pyrra any more than 20 minutes to fly there. They landed near the small village and since they did not know which house was the one they wanted, Angus decided to go into a petrol station that seemed to be the post office and local shop as well.

"Excuse me?" he asked the man behind the counter. "Can you tell me how to get to Long Reach House please?"

The man behind the counter was slightly balding with grey hair and looked as if he had been sleeping before Angus came in. His bushy eyebrows came together as he took Angus in with his bluish grey eyes.

"What would you want up there then?" enquired the old man.

Angus had not expected this and after a moment's silence, stammered out a hasty reply.

"Em…eh…I have a meeting with Mr Tek" he lied.

"Ah you're after him eh? Well not to worry, I was just making sure you're not one of them hooligans that go about vandalising other people's property. You can never be too careful nowadays." Without waiting for a reply from Angus he walked to the shop window and pointed up the road. "It's just up there on the right. Seen him about the other day but I don't know if he is still there now. Tell him he still has his grocery bill to pay when you see him."

"Thanks," piped Angus quickly and hurried out of the shop and across the road to where Pyrra waited for him. The old man watched Angus walk behind a tree and then.....nothing! He watched for a few seconds more and wondered why the boy was hiding behind the tree trunk. Thinking this was very odd, the old man walked across the road to the tree and walked around the other side. Then he walked round again. He stood scratching his bald head for a minute or two with a completely confused look on his face. He looked up and down the street again then walked back to his shop muttering about seeing things and dreaming up customers. He didn't hear the flapping of a pair of great green wings as he walked back to his shop.

Pyrra touched down on a large lawn that was clearly neglected.

"That was close Pyrra, for a second I thought he had seen us!"

They had swept past the main entrance and saw a worn and faded name plaque that confirmed that they had the correct house. Angus jumped down and looked around at the overgrown bushes and rhododendrons. The gate they had flown over had dragons on the gate posts and the house appeared un-kempt and as neglected as the garden. Angus walked towards the big house and taking a deep breath, rang the door bell. He was not really surprised when it did not work. He banged on the large front door and waited for what seemed like ages. Still nothing moved and still no-one answered. Walking round to the back of the house he took out his piece of ore from the pouch around his neck and looked at it to see if there were any dragons in the vicinity. The stone began to glow and Angus looked up thinking that a dragon was hiding nearby, waiting for him to find it. Just then Pyrra walked around the corner and saw him looking at the stone. It was her that the Dragonore was picking up and she called to him.

"There are no dragons here Angus, as I would feel their presence otherwise."

Angus reluctantly had to agree. He was extremely disappointed by not finding a dragon either in hiding by choice, or held against its will. They were both anxious to find anything that would help their search for the stranger.

"What do you want to do now then Angus, shall we go back?"

"Actually Miss Puttick thinks she has worked out another hiding place. Can we go and try that first?"

Due to Miss Puttick's efficient detective work in the library, Pyrra and Angus soon found themselves in the yard of a town pub in Marmiton, amongst stacks of metal beer barrels and plastic crates, presumably just delivered by the brewery.

"Stay here Pyrra and I'll run round to the front with the Dragonore and see if Cyru is hiding in the sign," said Angus making for the door into the pub, "and don't touch that stuff!" he added, seeing Pyrra sniffing one of the barrels curiously. He turned down the corridor and was about halfway along when the barman stopped him.

"Oi, you're not old enough to be in here youngster, you should be in the beer garden with your parents."

"Sorry," said Angus. "I'm looking for my Dad...he went off to the gents."

"OK straight through the lounge then, first door on the right."

Angus found himself in a dingy room with beer stained carpets and he headed straight for the main door by the windows before anyone else could stop him. Once out on the pavement he looked up and was right underneath the pub sign which proudly pictured 'The Blue Dragon'. 'This has to be Cyru' Angus thought and he touched the stone at his chest which felt only slightly warm. He called up to the sign,

"Hello... Cyru... Are you awake?"

Nothing remarkable happened and there was no change to the temperature of the mineral. It seemed to be only a faint signal as if a dragon had been in the sign, but nothing stirred within the picture. It just creaked and swayed on its bracket overhead.

Just then a few families started to gather outside the pub and Angus overheard their conversation. Two men were talking about the pub's social side, The Blue Dragons. They were playing a friendly football match on a nearby football field against their old rivals, The Queens Arms. 'That's where he'll be!' thought Angus 'Pyrra said he loved sport and crowds. He's probably their mascot or something silly like that'. There was no time to tell Pyrra and Angus hoped she'd stay quietly in the yard. He would have to follow the supporters or he'd never find where the game was being played. He set off briskly down the road.

Angus caught them up, but decided to stay just a little bit behind the main crowd. They walked between the shops at the end of the street, turning to follow an alley which brought them out behind the buildings. They crossed a stream and then strolled up a path which took them through a gate and onto a playing field. Angus managed to blend in easily as there were quite a few children around. As he walked through the gathering crowd he could hear most of the men of the town chatting amiably; discussing tactics and who was the best player. The two town pubs seemed to take the football very seriously and the rivalry was clearly apparent as they chanted intermittently at each other. Angus could now see a team in blue warming up and when they took off their tracksuit tops he could see a blue dragon logo on their football shirts. This was definitely the right sort of place to find Cyru then but the Dragonore was cold and showed no signs of life. Angus looked about and was half expecting the morphed blue dragon to appear and acknowledge the cheering crowd at the start of the game, just like any mascot. Of course this was no serious league game, just a small town social, so no mascots took to the pitch and Angus quickly lost interest. It seemed there were no dragons to be found here, and the ore continued to stay cold and dull as if to confirm his doubts.

He found his way back to the pub, darting past the barman when he was not looking and was amazed to see Pyrra lying inelegantly on her back, lapping up a pool of beer that she had somehow managed to spill out from a barrel. She was looking a bit sleepy and gave the equivalent of a dragon hiccup.

"Good stuff thish, Angush!"

"It should be, it's Dragon Ale" Angus read the label as he righted the barrel. He was amused and slightly appalled at the sight of a tipsy dragon.

"Pyrra how much of this did you drink?"

"Not mush (hic), jush a little dribble to get a tashte."

"You've drunk a whole barrel Pyrra! How do you feel?" Angus was now getting frustrated. Firstly he couldn't find Cyru and now Pyrra looked incapable of flying. How were they going to get home and where else could they look for Cyru? He was sure that the blue dragon had been here until quite recently. The pub sign did faintly register something with the Dragonore but there was no dragon around now. Well not a sober one at any rate.

"Pyrra come on. We need to go. Get up," he encouraged as she rolled about in the yard. She managed to haul herself up onto all fours and Angus wondered about the wisdom of a dragon taking off when she'd had too much beer.

"Have you ever tasted alcohol before?"

"Try shome Angus, its lovely!" she giggled, but Angus declined. He steered her away from the barrels and held three fingers up in front of her face. She seemed to be focusing. They'd have to take a chance.

"Okay look Pyrra we have to go. Pull yourself together. Cyru wasn't there although it seemed like a dragon had been once." Seeing that his statement had grabbed the dragon's attention he continued. "It could be that we have the wrong place though. I mean, it doesn't indicate that anything bad has happened to him. Does it?"

"Well Angush it's hard to think right now. My head hurts too much. Let's go home."

The flight home turned out to be a bit bumpy, mainly due to Pyrra's hiccups and she had to land several times because she felt sick. One stop amused Angus greatly and he started to giggle when Pyrra said.

"Angush I am shorry but I need to shtop again."

"Not again! Pyrra we will never get home at this rate. Can't it wait?"

"Nooo... It can't..." she actually looked embarrassed. "I think I drank far too much."

"Never... really... You...drink too much...I can't believe that!" teased Angus. Pyrra was not in the mood as she was now desperate.

"Stop it, I'm going down. I really need to go wee-wee." Angus could not believe what he had just heard and burst out laughing. He laughed so hard that his eyes were watering and he didn't see that Pyrra had landed lightly onto the ground. He jumped down and finally managed to ask.

"Why do you call it that?"

"That's what I hear the children say to their parents and I was trying to be polite. Now if you don't mind…"

Angus took the hint and turned away politely, walking away a little. He decided not to try and continue any serious conversation with her in her present state and they eventually landed without much grace, but at least unseen, in the trees around the corner where Angus got off and walked to the sweet shop. Pyrra flew to the plinth and quickly morphed back down to size. She closed her eyes and folded her wings around her like a comfort blanket.

"I think you better hurry up and go Angus," whispered Pyrra "I think I'm going to be sick!"

Angus decided to do as he was told. He'd never seen a dragon being sick and certainly didn't want to watch.

"No talking to strange men," he added cautiously, knowing however that she wouldn't. Suddenly she blinked her eyes open again and called him back remembering something important that she meant to tell him earlier.

"Do you remember what Godroi and Argent told us about the Loch Ness Monster? Well I think we should pay her a visit. She needs a friendly reminder that it doesn't do for one to be so careless. It endangers the lives of all the hidden dragons."

"Wow I'm up for that!" enthused Angus. "Do you really think that Nessie is a dragon?"

"She might be Angus and the only way to find out is to go and see for ourselves."

"Scotland here we come! I need to report to Miss Puttick tomorrow and tell her what's been happening!" he said more to himself. Angus sauntered down the High Street with his hands casually in his pockets and secretly bursting with inner excitement, leaving the dragon looking decidedly greener than usual.

Chapter 9

'Nathair'

Angus woke up on Sunday with his head full of questions. He was struggling to reason why anyone would want to take a dragon away from the safety of its shell. More so, who was it that had been visiting them and who had answered his letter? It made sense Rathlin was the one who had come to see him, since he was the only Mr Tek left. However Dermot had made it clear that Rathlin had no interest in dragons whatsoever. Could it be that someone else was pretending to be Finian? Was it likely that others could have come across the notes and information that Finian had left behind? He was still troubling over these questions when his Dad asked him to help him check the stock of the Kleanware products that had just arrived the day before. He had to put the thoughts out of his head until later because it took all day Sunday to sort out the mountains of cleaning products taking over the house and garage.

Back in the library the next morning, which seemed to have become the unofficial and amateur branch of the SSDP, Angus told Miss Puttick all about the unfruitful trip to Long Reach and the Blue Dragon pub. He tactfully left out Pyrra's beer tasting session, but he did tell her about their proposed trip to Loch Ness. Since she did not have any other leads for him the conversation stayed on Nessie.

"Ah yes, the Loch Ness Monster" said Miss Puttick "I've been reading about her recent antics in the newspapers. There has been a lot of activity in the loch and a spate of sightings. Apparently many experts are assembling at the loch as we speak. It seems they are on the verge of a breakthrough and believe they are close to revealing the truth about the legendary monster. I didn't give it much thought, but does Pyrra really think Nessie is a dragon?"

"She doesn't know for sure, but we're off to try and find out. Pyrra's worried that if she is about to be discovered it could cause problems for all hibernating dragons."

Tuesday morning Angus woke up early and looked out his window at what was shaping up to be a very wet day. He packed accordingly and left a note for his Mum that he was going out with a friend for the day and would be back at teatime. He didn't wait to tell her in person as he knew he would get roped into more Kleanware chores. He arrived at the sweet shop and not surprisingly Pyrra still had a headache. Angus tried to get her to take some tablets that he knew his Mum took, but the dragon was not willing to take them and was moaning a lot.

"Oh I don't want to ever drink again," groaned Pyrra once they were in the air. "I still don't feel too well."

"It serves you right... I did warn you not to."

Pyrra went quiet and hung her head feeling sorry for herself. Angus decided to tell her what he had been thinking about for the last two days.

"If you are correct in your supposition that Rathlin Tek has taken Cyru then where would he have taken him?" questioned Pyrra after Angus had told her his theories.

"Well we know Cyru is not at Long Reach so he must be in Calmor Castle," Angus scratched his head, "but if he was at the castle when we were there, wouldn't we have known?"

"It depends on how close we were to him and we couldn't have done anything about it then could we?" said Pyrra rubbing her forehead. "At least not with those hounds running about."

"It doesn't make any sense though as I was in the castle and felt nothing from the ore... Besides what would Rathlin want dragons for anyway?" said Angus.

"I don't know, but from previous experience whenever humans get involved with dragons it doesn't usually end up in our favour," said Pyrra anxiously.

"The problem is we have no proof Pyrra. For all we know Cyru might have been away flying or we just had the wrong place. It also might be someone else and Rathlin really isn't involved."

It was now pouring with rain and rather chilly despite being the height of summer. The two friends were quiet for some time, both deep in thought about who was behind the strange visits and why.

Angus had never been to Scotland where his grandfather came from, and was enjoying the sightseeing. He did up his hooded top against the driving rain and laughed as he remembered his Gran saying you don't go to Scotland for the weather! The countryside changed dramatically and lochs as glens whooshed by below them and the ground seemed a mass of purple heather. Pyrra was still feeling a little fragile and so they swerved and dipped perhaps a little more than usual for a dragon who had now regained the full strength of her wings.

Angus was still taking in the scenery when he heard a growling noise and felt a vibration from Pyrra's body.

"What was that, Pyrra?"

"Angus I have to make another stop."

"What for… is there something wrong?"

"Well not exactly… It's because I am no longer in hibernation, you see…I'm hungry."

"Oh, right, I never thought about that Pyrra… So what do dragons eat?"

"I was thinking one of those sheep looked just about right."

"Pyrra you can't! They belong to someone. That's stealing."

"It's not stealing," replied Pyrra indignantly. "One or two always die by natural causes. I'm just another small hazard… and I don't eat much. It's just the odd one every now and then."

"Pyrra you're not exactly what you could call a natural hazard," chuckled Angus in reply.

"Okay but at least I'm not a normal part of the food chain!" answered Pyrra indignantly.

"Well if you have to, but if you don't mind I won't look."

Pyrra flew down to a tree line below them and left Angus for about ten minutes. Secretly Angus thought it was pretty cool and imagined Pyrra swooping down on some unsuspecting sheep in the field before carrying it off for dinner. Just then Pyrra returned and they were soon up in the sky again with Pyrra showing no signs of having eaten anything. Angus had at least expected to see her licking her lips or some other tell-tale sign of blood but there was nothing.

Pyrra started to follow a road and did so for sometime. Angus could see the cars on it. They were parked in the middle of the road and Angus couldn't help thinking that it looked very dangerous to stop like that. Then he realised that they were moving. Of course he had forgotten about dragon time and how it sped time up for the dragon in flight. At that, Angus' eyes seemed to blur as he stared at the slow motion vehicles. Suddenly they were moving at the same speed as Pyrra, and Angus realised that they must be nearly there. They rose over an impressive mountainside and came upon a long loch which seemed to stretch forever. The water was black and looked really deep. Angus thought it was a really cool place and was dying to stop to do some exploring. If only it wasn't for the rain! He was soaked through already. Pyrra seemed oblivious to his discomfort. Obviously thick dragon scales are quite waterproof!

Angus and Pyrra circled over Loch Ness and eventually spied a statue of the Loch's most famous inhabitant; Nessie.

"That looks like a likely spot Angus and my Dragonore tells me that is no ordinary statue... Hold on and I will take us down."

"If Nessie is a dragon and causing all the commotion in the loch, does that mean you can swim as well, Pyrra?"

"I can swim but most dragons do not normally like water. If this is a dragon, and I think it is, then it is most likely a Wyrm."

"A Wyrm?" repeated Angus.

"Yes a water dragon. They don't fly as they prefer water."

"WOW! Do you really think that a water dragon could be hiding in that statue?" Angus asked his scaly friend.

"No doubt about it... the perfect habitat for a slimy snake-like serpent... close to water's edge."

Pyrra landed deftly on the shore, unseen by the tourists. Most of them were scanning the murky depths of the loch with small children convinced they could see a monster, but usually it turned out to be a passing duck or wooden log.

Invisible to the crowds and armed with his precious piece of Dragonore, Angus confronted the statue and tried to awaken Nessie.

"OK Pyrra let me try and do this on my own. I think I'm getting the hang of this now" the boy said confidently. He made his approach but nothing happened. "What am I doing wrong?" he asked his bemused dragon friend. Pyrra replied,

"I think she can hear you but she's ignoring you for some reason. Maybe she doesn't trust you. Let me speak to her."

There followed a brief exchange in what could only be described as 'dragon' and suddenly a dark brown slimy sea-serpent morphed on the grass next to a stunned Angus, but completely unseen by the tourists. Although the beast had a dragon's head it was long and snake-like with small gills and appeared to be always moving. In fact Angus decided it was sort of shifty and he wasn't sure why but he had an inexplicable uneasy feeling about it.

"He says his name is Nathair and he's MALE!"

"Nessie is a boy!" exclaimed Angus.

"Aye I am, an' am fed up being called Nessie an' al thank yi no tae forget it" interrupted Nathair.

"He's a water dragon and only leaves the safety of his shell when he thinks he can get away with it. He loves to swim in the loch despite the cold," continued Pyrra.

"A find it quite invigorating ye ken, an' a thought this would be a great place tae hide. Av been here for hundreds of years" he told Angus in his strange serpent like Scottish accent. "Every noo an' then ssomeone thinks they ssee me an' then there's a flurry of interest with busloads of tourists an' film crews keeping vigil at the loch sside, that's when a hide until it aw dies doun again."

"But...they said it was all fake!" replied an incredulous Angus.

"Och av sseen yon eejits tying auld tyres together way rope and floating them on the water trying tae fool folks."

"Has anyone been up here recently with Dragonore" asked Pyrra.

Nathair just hissed at Pyrra in a rather unfriendly manner as if to say 'mind your own business,' which Angus took to mean no.

"Av got ma little dips doon tae a fine art," boasted the water dragon in his bizarre accent. "Naebody knows aboot me an' they'll never discover ma little ssecret."

"You really should be more careful Nathair" Pyrra frowned. "You will make it difficult for other dragons if you get caught."

"Dinnae fas yersel wummin!" barked Nathair. "A just ssend a few ripples oot now an' then tae gie thon tourists whit they come tae ssee. Then a ssneak back tae shore using ma neat camouflage an' morph back intae ma hidey hole…. Look al show you how a dae it…" and before Angus and Pyrra could say anything the slippery serpent slid down the bank and entered the inky black water. He barely broke the surface of the loch before diving down into the murky depths.

Unbeknown to the dragons or the boy, a team of 'experts' had been tailing what they believed to be 'Nessie' for months. The headstrong Wyrm had been a bit careless of late and was not quite as invisible as he thought. As the water dragon shimmied along the bottom of the Loch, he was quite oblivious to the large net which was just below the surface at the end of the loch, just where he had entered the water. He was swimming into a trap!

Suddenly Angus spotted a couple of frogmen, with just their heads visible on top of the water, pulling on ropes to tighten the net. They hoped one way or another to solve the Loch Ness monster phenomenon once and for all. Angus pointed the divers out to Pyrra, but he was not overly concerned as he thought the wily water dragon would quickly morph back into the statue at the first hint of trouble.

"But he can't!" cried Pyrra, realising the danger that Nathair was in. "He has to be on dry land to morph, he can't do it in the water! What are we going to do?"

Quick as a flash Angus formulated a plan and jumped on the flustered Pyrra's back.

"Fly as fast as you can to the middle of the loch, away from the net" shouted Angus.

When he was satisfied that they were far enough away from the trapped water dragon, Angus took off his backpack, put his precious Dragonore inside it and handed it forward to Pyrra.

"Look after that" was all he said.

Before she could reply he jumped off her back and plummeted down to the dark and very uninviting water below. If anyone had been watching they would have been amazed to see an eleven-year-old boy suddenly appear out of thin air, falling from the sky and landing with a big splash in the murky water of Loch Ness.

Without the protection of Dragonore and Pyrra's company, Angus was fully visible and it was his intention to draw the focus of the crowd away from the net. This gave the trapped water dragon enough time to escape to the shore. What Angus had not bargained for was the freezing temperature of the water, despite it being an August day. The cold water hit him like a slap and he didn't have to fake the panic in his voice as he flayed about quite helplessly, all arms and legs, gulping the freezing cold water and literally fearing for his life. Immediately the people in the boats turned their attention to the drowning boy, shouting to the divers to rescue him as they were already in the water. The frogmen left the ropes and quickly swam to the distressed boy, hoisting him out of the water and depositing the spluttering and shaking lad on the bank.

Watching the drama unfold from invisible safety, Pyrra shouted to the frightened water dragon to find a way out of the net. Now the ropes had been slackened the dragon could free himself and get out of the water whilst everyone's eyes were on poor Angus. Nathair didn't need telling twice. He escaped the floating net and slithered out of the water onto the shore and morphed back into the statue known as 'Nessie'.

Angus was meanwhile bundled up in blankets and being plied with reviving hot broth from a flask. His main concern was how to get away from the scene unnoticed. People were already talking about getting a newspaper reporter down and they asked him where his parents were. Somehow he had to get away from the attention! The near capture of 'Nessie' was not completely forgotten in the wake of the dramatic rescue. The scientists started to argue again about the existence of the monster and taking advantage of the commotion, Angus dropped the blankets. He slipped to the ground and dove through the thronging legs before scampering to the statue where he spied his abandoned backpack, just where Pyrra had dropped it. His cold hands fumbled with the zip as he needed the Dragonore to enable him to see Pyrra and to disappear. At last his frozen fingers closed around the stone and it glowed warm in his hand. There she was, relieved to see he was okay and she beckoned him over. He clambered onto her back and spread his shivering body over the great green scaly back enjoying the feeling of warmth coursing through his veins.

"I was so worried about you," she chided. "That was a very brave thing to do. You saved that foolish wyrm's life and by doing so upheld one of the oaths of the dragon protectors!"

They circled the statue and just saw the brown forked tail disappearing as Nathair morphed back into the statue.

"I think it will be a while before Nathair takes to the water again!" remarked Pyrra. "Ungrateful creature... not a word of thanks... and his foolish actions nearly exposed us all to the world!"

"W... w... well at le... at least he didn't have any visit... ors" stuttered Angus, who was now shivering in the wind as Pyrra flew south.

"Hold on Angus we are going down for a minute."

Pyrra quickly spiralled down to a small wooded area and told Angus to stay on her back and hug her tightly. Pyrra closed her eyes and heat began to radiate from her body. Angus couldn't believe it he felt much better as the heat from Pyrra warmed his clothes and his body, drying him out.

"Thanks Pyrra that was brilliant!"

"You're welcome Angus and hopefully you will feel much better for the flight home."

"What did you do?" asked Angus.

"It's an old trick," she laughed. "I had to land as it takes all my concentration to do that and I was therefore visible again. We can go home now if you like."

"Yes please Pyrra, I've had enough adventure for one day."

"You almost sounded like Miss Puttick" laughed the dragon.

Pyrra gathered herself and with a mighty beat of her wings launched herself into the air and set off homewards. Little did either of them know that the papers the next day would be full of stories about a mysterious disappearing boy!

Chapter 10

'Unwelcome Visitor'

Angus had a cold.

"Can't think where you got that from," chided his mother on her way out of the front door piled up with Kleanware boxes. 'If only she knew!' thought Angus. She tried to confine him indoors but he convinced her that a bike ride in the beautiful warm sunshine was just what he needed and he set off to find Pyrra.

Pleased to see her new friend quite recovered, apart from his runny nose, Pyrra shared with Angus the news that Godroi had given her about Rhys, and where they might find her.

"Have you been off to see him without me?" teased Angus.

Pyrra ignored him and looked away shyly, then she continued.

"There was a beautiful place, a long time ago, in the grounds of an old house. It had a secret lake covered with water lilies and edged with weeping willow trees, trailing their branches in the still and silent water. It's a contemplative place of absolute calm, with the silence only broken by the occasional birdsong." She looked wistfully into space and Angus asked,

"Have you been there?"

"Eh… Oh… Only the once but it was a long time ago. I can't remember the exact spot. I remember that behind the secret lake, there is a garden where the air is heavy with the scent of old-fashioned roses and the rockeries are brimming with lavender and heartsease. The borders are alive with the droning of hundreds of nectar-laden bees and the fluttering of butterfly wings, which adds to the serenity and richness of the garden. Rhys loved it there more than any other earthly place, and that's where Godroi thinks she may be found."

"That could be anywhere really. Was there anything else that might help Miss Puttick work out the location?"

"Well Godroi did mention that on top of the roof of the house, towering over the twisted Elizabethan chimney pots, there is an unusual weather vane with a dragon instead of the more common cockerel."

"Wow, is Rhys on the roof then, hiding in the weather vane?" asked Angus.

"No she's in the garden in the guise of a statue" said Pyrra.

"So there may be another dragon up on the roof then?" Angus persisted.

"Yes, quite possibly, but we won't know until we get there. First we need to find out where this house is."

"Okay I'll go and see Miss Puttick" said Angus, not sure what she would make of these clues. He cycled home as fast as he could.

Miss Puttick, who loved a challenge, listened to his description of the garden, and the house with the strange weathervane.

"Right, let's do a search on the Internet" she said. "But what are we looking for?" asked Angus.

"Weathervanes," said Miss Puttick as she clicked onto a search engine. "Let me see, weathervanes... peacock, unicorn, spider, ah! Here we go... dragon weather vane... Mapleton House... Here's the address. Pass the Route Finder." It was as easy as that and Angus was impressed.

Not long afterwards Angus found himself in the middle of the most beautiful English rose garden you could imagine, and on the edge of a secret lake, just as Pyrra had described. The hazy Thursday afternoon air was warm with summer sunshine and lazy with the buzzing of a thousand bees. There was an overwhelming scent from wild roses and other sweet smelling blooms with a heady mixture of lavender, alyssum and honeysuckle that produced a uniquely English summer smell. This garden felt close to paradise and it was no wonder a dragon would choose to hibernate here!

Angus looked around taking it all in. Then he saw it. In the middle of the rose garden, surrounded by a ring of sweet smelling alyssum, Angus spied a mossy statue. Rushing over to it, he found himself face to face with a serene, if somewhat lichen-covered replica of a dragon with a rather wistful look on its face. The Dragonore glowed on his chest and warmed

at his touch confirming his suspicions. He had indeed found Rhys.

"Over here Pyrra! Quick I've found her!" he shouted.

Meanwhile Pyrra was also enjoying breathing in the scents of the flowers and was teasing the bees by scorching them gently with her hot but not fiery breath. She came over to see what her friend had found.

"Well, well...Rhys you beautiful creature, it's me, Pyrra," she breathed.

"We mean you no harm" said Angus, willing the dragon statue to respond.

"For goodness sake Angus, we're dragons, not aliens" teased Pyrra. "If you'd addressed me in that fashion I would never have woken up!"

The garden dragon shook her head a few times, much like a woman shakes down her long hair, and before Angus' eyes she morphed into a stunning red dragon as she gracefully stepped off the plinth.

"My, the years have been good to you!" Pyrra murmured as the two dragons appeared to kiss cheeks.

"Do you have any news of the others?" asked Rhys in a deep and gorgeous velvet voice. She listened intently as Pyrra related the tale of how they had found Godroi and Argent, and of course, why Angus was there. He stood doing goldfish impressions, quite stunned by the red dragon and wondered if he would ever get used to watching the dragons. He had fallen completely under her spell. Her voice and manner were very compelling. No wonder Pyrra and Rhys had been rivals for the affections of Godroi and Argent. However despite her great beauty, listening to Rhys Angus found her to be quite superior and haughty in manner and much preferred the livelier humour of Pyrra. He wondered if the male dragons felt the same.

Angus wandered around the garden looking up at the house and he spied the unusual weathervane; which indeed had a dragon on the top, just as described. Angus pointed it out and asks Rhys if that was perhaps the hiding place of another dragon.

"Alas it was" she said sadly, "A young dragon, I never found out his name. He was a boastful fellow and wasn't afraid of anything, even the most terrific thunderstorms. He had been hit by lightning and survived. Rather thought himself a bit indestructible."

"What happened to him?" enquired Angus.

"I did try to warn him but he just wouldn't listen and seemed to delight in trying to frighten me with his daring deeds. He decided to make the weathervane his alter shell and unfortunately he got struck by lightning three times in one night. It was a terrible storm and that was the end of him."

"Was that recently?" asked Angus curiously.

"Oh a few hundred years ago," said Rhys as if it was only yesterday.

Angus privately thought he'd call the unlucky dragon 'Toast' as that appealed to his sense of humour. The two female dragons were busily reminiscing in falsetto voices and he was as disinterested as he was when Pyrra was flirting with the male dragons. Pyrra broke into his thoughts, as Rhys was telling her something important.

"There was a man here, with Dragonore who tried to get me to go with him," breathed the gorgeous red dragon, huskily. "He told me he could protect me at his home, remote and safe from mankind, a place where I could live safely, away from the dangers of the world. He also told me he could get me Blue Dragon Fire. I listened to his fine words, tempted at first, but even despite the offer of Blue Dragon Fire, I didn't trust him. There was just something about him. So I stayed silent and hidden, not showing myself to him at all."

"Did he have a ponytail?" asked Angus.

"He had a hood and wore a long black coat so I can't tell you. What he wanted with me I don't know either, but he did say he knew a friend of mine, a blue dragon, which could only mean Cyru if you've already found the others."

"This is really bad Pyrra. We were too late to find Cyru and that strange man now says he has him. It has to be the same man who came to see me."

"You may be right Angus," said Pyrra, "but whoever he is, he's found the four of us for definite and he must have found Cyru as well. Knowing Cyru as I do, I fear he would have been gullible enough to be taken in by this man's promises."

They took their leave of Rhys who, with a toss of her beautiful dragonhead, morphed back into the garden statue once more as the anxious pair returned to Piggleston.

Arriving back home, Angus was not really surprised to find the house empty. His parents were obviously out and about with their Kleanware business. He had just finished making himself a sandwich and was about to cycle round to the library when he heard a loud knock at the front door. Angus stowed his bike against the back wall of the house and went into the hall. When he looked through the front door he could see a tall dark figure behind the smoked glass and grabbing the handle he opened the door.

"Hi can I help y...ou?" he had nearly frozen as he had looked up into the face of the visitor. The man was older than the portrait Angus had seen but there was no mistaking who it was standing in front of him. He hoped he had not given himself away to the man now on his doorstep.

"Hello young man, my name is Rathlin Tek. I am looking for Angus Munro. Would that be you?" he smiled. Angus recognised Rathlin straight away as the man who had been talking to Pyrra in the High Street. He had the same coat on and his hair was the same colour. From this angle it looked slicked back but Angus would bet his Dragonore that it was tied in a ponytail.

"Yes it's me you want... but how do you know about me?"

"Ah yes. You wrote a letter to Finian, my brother. Unfortunately he died some time back and well... how shall I put it... I have carried on the family business if you like," he finished with an ingratiating smile.

Angus could see that he was trying to be charming, but Rathlin only reminded him of the slimy water dragon with its arrogant manner. Angus was tired and still feeling the after-effects of his cold but he was also very curious to know what the white-haired man wanted with him and the dragons. What Angus did not know was that Rathlin had seen him with Pyrra at Calmor. Foolishly Angus let the strange man into the house.

"You had better come in then," replied Angus, stepping aside to show the stranger into the hallway.

"I've come to see what you know about dragons, young man" smiled Rathlin while following Angus into the living room.

"You wrote to my late brother Finian a few weeks ago… and since good protectors are hard to find these days, I thought we should meet and discuss how we may help each other."

Angus looked into the smiling face of Rathlin, who had the rather smug look of someone who thought they had the upper hand. Angus decided to play along and try to find out about Cyru.

"Is it safe to talk Angus, as I would not want your parents to overhear our conversation?" As he said this Rathlin turned to look at the door leading to the hall and Angus caught a glimpse of the white ponytail, just as the dragons had described to him. His suspicions about Rathlin were correct after all.

"Yeah it's fine, they're out just now."

Rathlin just smiled wider than before.

"So Angus, tell me, have you seen any dragons?"

Instinct told Angus to keep quiet about Pyrra and he just shook his head.

"No I haven't. I did find the book that Finian wrote and that is where I got the message."

"Which message would that be?" enquired Rathlin.

"Oh the secret one that Finian left for the right kind of person to find," he answered truthfully, and certain that Rathlin had not found it. "That's where I got the address of Long Reach and I wrote the letter to Finian."

Rathlin seemed to lose a little of his composure. Obviously not knowing about the pamphlet was a concern to him. He quickly smiled again and asked,

"This... message, do you have it here?"

"Sorry... No... It's in the library, inside the book... I wasn't allowed to take it out," he lied.

"Not to worry. Maybe I can visit the library and see it for myself... So you were saying that you had seen a dragon then?"

"Em... No... I said I had not seen a dragon."

"So you don't believe in them then?"

"I didn't say that!" replied Angus quickly.

"Well you can't be a protector if you don't believe and if you don't believe you can't see them," replied Rathlin with a smirk on his face.

"You can see them if you have dragono..!"

Angus froze in horror. He had not meant to say anything about the stone but he wanted to remove the smug look from the interrogator's face. He looked at

Rathlin, who in turn was studying Angus, his shining eyes and smile portrayed a triumphant look and Angus knew he had slipped up.

"Dragonore did you say? Now how would you know that to be true?" When Angus did not answer right away Rathlin continued.

"You see I have seen my brother's book and although I did not find any secret messages, I do know that he explains about Dragonore and the reason you believe in it, is because you have used it!" He paused for a second weighing Angus up and then continued,

"So I will ask you again young man. How and what do you know about dragons, and Dragonore?"

Angus was feeling very uncomfortable and now wished he hadn't let Rathlin into his house. Sensing the silence to mean Angus was digging his heels in, Rathlin changed tack.

"Look Angus, if you are to be a protector, then you will have to be honest with me. I cannot help you meet dragons if I cannot trust you."

Rathlin was smiling again and Angus just wanted him to go but instead he asked.

"How many dragons do you have?"

"Well I have one at the minute, a nice blue one in fact, but with your help Angus I could help many more. At least four, don't you think?"

Angus held his breath. He did not want to give anything away and hoped that he had kept his face emotionless when Rathlin made that last statement. The white haired visitor stared at him intently, waiting for him to reply and Angus, realising his insecure situation, was getting more and more worried. Despite this, Angus decided to push his luck a little bit more.

"Wow you have a blue dragon! I wish I had one, can I see him? Where is he?" he exclaimed with feigned interest. Rathlin's smile disappeared and his eyes narrowed angrily.

"You think me a fool boy!" he scolded.

Angus could see that Rathlin was now incensed and that he had gone too far.
The situation was getting more frightening and now he just wanted to get the man out of the house. He wished Miss Puttick was there.

"Do you wish to test me? I want to know about the dragon you have been seeing. Tell me what you know NOW!" he bellowed the last word making Angus jump. Angus stood up and said,

"I think it is time for you to go n…"

Rathlin jumped to his feet and grabbed Angus by the neck of his t-shirt.

"You're lying to me boy! Now tell me the truth… I've seen you… I must have that dragon," he spat and raised his fist.

Just then, a key rattled in the lock of the front door.

"Cooey! Angus, come and help me with this stuff will you" shouted a familiar voice.

Angus had never been so pleased to see his Mum in all his life. Not that he could, as she was piled up with boxes. Rathlin instantly let go and shoved the boy back onto the sofa. He strode out of the room, barging past Angus' Mum as he fled. She got such a shock she dropped the boxes of Kleanware cloths all over the hall. Angus heard her scream, jumped up and ran to see what had happened. Seeing that his Mum was okay he looked out
the door to see where Rathlin went, but there was no sign of him. Angus turned back to help his Mum. She looked really cross.

"Who on earth was that then?"

"Just a friend Mum, he had to go and he is really shy. I'm sorry he made you drop the boxes."

"You didn't tell me you were bringing a friend of yours round dear. Very rude of him to rush off like that, I must say," she said indignantly.

"I'm sorry Mum. I will tell him off the next time I see him."

"Be a dear and put the kettle on would you?" she asked, taking her shoes off. Angus finished helping his Mum pick up the scattered goods. His mind was racing as he went to make the tea. He's seen me with Pyrra? When? How? He has a dragon already? He was sure now that Rathlin was the man who had been questioning the other dragons…but how did he know of their whereabouts? Of course! Rathlin is the owner of Calmor Castle and he must have worked out the significance of the wall paintings in the Great Hall! He also owned Long Reach in Lower Dinton; the old man in the shop told him as much. It was all finally fitting into place.

"Cyru, he has Cyru!" said Angus out loud.

"See who?" queried his Mum as she entered the kitchen.

"Oh nothing Mum," replied Angus quickly and busied himself with making the tea.

Angus knew he needed the help of Miss Puttick as she would know what to do. They would obviously have to go to Calmor Castle again and see if they could find out what had become of poor Cyru, as the dragon was obviously not at Long Reach. Rathlin was dangerous and Angus knew this by the way he had grabbed him. What he wanted with dragons was anybody's guess, but Angus was certain it was not for their protection.

He had to talk to the others quickly.

Chapter 11

'Calmor's Secret'

Angus cycled to Piggleston in record time as he knew he had to make sure that Pyrra wasn't in danger and arrived quite out of breath. People were starting to go home and the High Street was emptying. Luckily Pyrra was alone and she listened to the boy's spluttered ramblings.

"Now, now Angus calm down and tell me slowly."

"It was Rathlin… Pyrra! I was right! He was at my house and… at first he… was… friendly but then he turned… nasty and attacked me!" he said breathlessly.

"HE WHAT!" she bellowed, making Angus check to see if anyone had heard. Then he remembered they did not have Dragonore.

"Are you hurt? Tell me everything Angus and leave nothing out" she commanded.

Angus told her every single detail he could recall and waited for Pyrra's reply.

"Meet me at the trees Angus, we need to speak to Miss Puttick about this, as I think we need her help."

Pyrra touched down at the trees and did not waste any time.

"Right get on my back. You can show me the way to the library. We have to put an end to this matter as soon as we can" she said as she took off again in one stride.

Pyrra was tired as she had not flown so much since before her hibernation, but knew she had to somehow find the strength for yet another long journey. Sensing her fatigue, but also her concern for Cyru's wellbeing, Angus said,

"Pyrra, you're exhausted, I'll cycle home and catch Miss P in the library and you can rest a bit. We'll come back for you when we're ready to go."

"No Angus we need her to know now. If anything happens to you, or me, then it would be best that someone else knows what is going on; and for the sake of Cyru we cannot waste any time."

Pyrra picked up Angus' bike and they flew the short distance to the Library, in no time at all. Miss Puttick had just locked up. Angus gave her a brief explanation of his encounter with Rathlin Tek and his discovery about Cyru.

"Oh Angus, that was very foolish, you could have been hurt."

"I know, but I had to find out about Cyru and it worked out in the end. It was just as well Mum came back when she did though."

"He cannot have gone far," said Pyrra. "I think we should go back to Long Reach House and see if he is there."

"Yes I think you are probably right Pyrra, but when are we going to go?"

"Now... like I said to Angus, we have no time to waste." Angus jumped up onto Pyrra's back and invited Miss Puttick up.

"I can see I have no choice in the matter" she nervously laughed as she climbed up behind Angus.

They landed in the overgrown garden as before and Angus immediately ran to the building with his Dragonore fetched from its pouch. After several minutes of banging on doors and windows, repeatedly checking and re-checking the Dragonore, it was obvious that no-one was there. It was also clear to them what the next step was.

"He's not here Pyrra. He must have gone back to Calmor."

"I think you are right Angus. We can only hope that he is holding Cyru there and that we will be able to free him."

"Could it be that Cyru has chosen to stay at Calmor?" asked Miss Puttick nervously wringing her left hand with the right.

"It is possible, but I think it unlikely. My instinct tells me that Cyru is, or will be in danger, and we need to help him." replied Pyrra.

"So what are we waiting for?" shouted Angus.

"We can't go now, Angus" replied Miss Puttick, "We will have to go tomorrow. It's already far too late and your parents need not be any more troubled than they probably already are."

"Miss Puttick is correct Angus. We will travel first thing in the morning, and then we will sort out this Rathlin Tek fellow, once and for all" agreed Pyrra.

They were soon at the library and both Pyrra and Angus bade Miss Puttick goodnight. As she strode off around the corner Angus turned to Pyrra,

"What if he comes back tonight? What if he comes back for you, Pyrra?"

"Then he will save me a trip to Calmor and I will be able to deal with him all the sooner."

Angus could see that she was angry and he did not like to think of what she could do to Rathlin. Sensing the concern in her young friend Pyrra said,

"Do not worry about me Angus I will be fine. Now go home and sleep and we will meet here in the morning."

The two friends said goodnight and Angus watched as Pyrra flew off back to Piggleston. He was worried. Rathlin was not stupid and Angus knew that he was not the type of man that would let things get in his way. Angus had read many adventure books about people like that and could only hope that Rathlin would be beaten like the baddies he had read about. Only the problem was that the books he read were fiction and this was real life. In real life things didn't always happen the way you wanted them to. He cycled home and spent a sleepless night full of nightmarish dreams about Pyrra being in trouble.

Miss Puttick arrived at the library the next morning to find Angus and Pyrra already waiting for her. Although she didn't relish the prospect of the long flight to Calmor, she could see that this time she had no choice. A dragon's life was possibly in danger and she could not stand idly by and see Angus go off with Pyrra to face this ghastly man. If anything happened to the boy, she would never forgive herself.

This time the flight to Calmor was incident-free, no gliders or anything else to cause them concern. They hardly spoke on the way, as all three were deep in their own thoughts about what they might find at Calmor. As they flew towards the island, Pyrra, like last time, had the feeling that she had visited this place in the long and hazy past, but so long ago that she could barely remember it. She wished that the fuzziness of her memories, which came from being so long in hibernation, would hurry up and lift so she could clearly recall all that she needed to.

The trio arrived on the shore as before. All seemed tranquil and not at all as sinister as they had expected. The Blue Dragon Fire was quivering in the summer breeze and giving off its familiar heady aniseed scent. They looked up towards the castle and could see the clouds were masking parts of it with a grey blanket as the sun brightened other areas. Angus had the feeling they were being watched, but could not see anyone about.

"We have to be really careful Pyrra, those dogs might be about," warned Angus.

"Just you leave the dogs to me Angus, I will deal with them in no time at all," she replied with a businesslike look on her face.

"Where do we start?" asked Miss Puttick.

"I think up there is as good a place as any" replied Angus and he set off up the hillside. Pyrra followed quickly to stay beside her eager young friend and Miss Puttick reluctantly brought up the rear, glancing around nervously. When they reached the top of the hill they could still see no sign of life and Angus touched his chest to feel the reassuring Dragonore. They walked slowly up to the great front doors unchallenged and all the time looking around as if expecting Rathlin to appear, urging his dogs to attack them. When this did not happen, Miss Puttick turned to Angus and Pyrra,

"Well, what now?"

Angus did not hesitate and he turned the great cast iron handle on the Celtic marked doors.

The doors swept open and apart from the crest above the fireplace Angus could make out nothing in the Great Hall beyond. He pushed the doors further for Pyrra and the trio entered the darkened Great Hall through the arched opening. Other than Pyrra's claws, making clipping noises on the flagstones, it was eerily silent. As they walked to the centre, Angus could see shafts of sunlight from the windows piercing the gloom, but he noticed that Pyrra's gaze was drawn to the other side of the Hall, where the murals he had described to her, adorned the wall in silence. They stopped, not really knowing what to do next and Angus could see that the place looked exactly the same as before. Well... almost! Lying against one wall, quite near where Godroi's painting hung, were more pictures. They were facing inwards and Angus walked over and pulled back the first one. It was just as he had thought.

"Pyrra look! More pictures of dragons."

"Clearly Rathlin is not content to have just one dragon and intends to track down as many as he can" said Pyrra.

"But why does he need so many dragons? Is he starting some sort of zoo or a theme park?" exclaimed Angus.

"Who kno... Good gracious me!" Miss Puttick's reply was cut short by a muffled howl.

"What was that?" asked Angus.

"One of the dogs I hope!" cried Miss Puttick.

"That was no dog" replied Pyrra, "it came from over here," she finished as she strode along the wall with the dragon paintings. Angus could see that she was heading for an open door that, had it been closed, would have been quite invisible.

"We never saw that the last time we were here, did we Angus?" said Miss Puttick warily.

Angus did not reply, because Pyrra had passed through the opening; which was again designed just large enough for a dragon to use and she had started to clamber down the stairs towards whatever awaited them at the bottom.

"Wait!" called Angus, "We can't see in the dark," he shouted as he bent and rummaged for torches in his backpack. He found what he was looking for and switched them on, handing one to Miss Puttick.

"That seems to be a magical bag Angus," chuckled Pyrra from below, "you always manage to find what you need in it."

"I just believe in being prepared, that's all," replied Angus bashfully.

They descended the stairs with Angus shining his torch in front of them and peered into the gloom as they went, scared of what they might meet at the bottom. In truth, the stairs were not that long and Angus soon found himself in a cellar with empty wine racks lined up along the walls. Shining his torch around the large cellar Angus could see a door at the other end. He watched Miss Puttick try to push it open once they reached it, but the door was locked and it didn't even seem to have a handle. Angus noticed that it had a very strange looking lock; more of a groove or a hole, but definitely nothing for a key to fit into.

"I've remembered something…" exclaimed Pyrra, "try putting your Dragonore into that groove."

Angus reluctantly fished out the stone from the pouch around his neck and placed it in the groove. Immediately they heard a whirring noise and a click. The door swung open and Angus quickly retrieved the precious Dragonore and held the door open with his foot for Miss Puttick and the dragon to follow him through. They found themselves in a wide and rough tunnel sloping downwards and a very cold draft swooped up along the corridor towards them.

"Watch your step!" shouted Angus as Miss Puttick stumbled over a loose bit of rock.

The path descended sharply and after a lot of scrambling and slipping they began to see the faint glow of daylight below them in the distance.

"I hope that's the bottom," Miss Puttick said anxiously as she slipped again for the fifth time, her sensible shoes not giving her much grip on the slippery stone floor.

When they reached the bottom they cautiously stepped into a large cave. In front of them and slightly to the right stood an opening that looked to be covered over with the Blue Dragon Fire on the outside. The rambling plant was letting the light in but Angus was certain it was also screening the cave from the outside world. A small jetty, cut from the rock, was to the front of where they were standing and although no boat could be seen there now, Angus could see that the jetty had been in regular use. Ropes lay coiled beside the cave walls and small cleats, used to tie up a boat, were fixed to the rock looking shiny, as if new. It looked like the only way in and out of the cave mouth was by boat... unless... 'Yes, I could just imagine a dragon flying through that entrance' thought Angus.

He was still pondering these thoughts when suddenly a terrible noise filled the chamber. It sounded like a badly wounded animal and was definitely the same cry they had heard from above, only this time much, much louder. As one they turned in the direction the sound had come from. Now Angus knew, judging by what stood in front of them, that his thoughts about dragons flying in and out the cave were correct.

A pair of giant oak doors, similar to the ones at the entrance to the castle, but about twice the size, was just about visible in the gloomy shadows.

"Tell me you heard that terrible noise?" whispered Miss Puttick.

"Come on," said Angus, "it could be Cyru. We need to find a way through these doors."

Slowly they approached the doors, moving forward to touch the large handles. Just as they did so, another howl erupted throughout the chamber!

"I can't tell who that is, but one thing I do know, is the sound of another dragon in distress."

Forgetting all about any fear they may have, they rushed to the door handles and pulled as hard as they could, but nothing happened. They tried pushing, but still nothing moved.

"Hold on is that another one of those Dragonore locks?" asked Miss Puttick.

"Yes! That's it… hold on and I'll try it," replied Angus fetching out his precious stone.

He pressed the ore into the slot and Miss Puttick pulled on the handles. Nothing moved! She pulled again but this time so hard that her face was flushed red and all screwed up. When she got no reaction to that, she tried to push, but again without any luck.

"It worked before so why not now?" asked a confused Angus.

"Perhaps there is some sort of magic at work that we do not know yet," replied Pyrra.

Then Angus noticed some more small carvings on the oak.

"Pyrra I can't read this, can you?"

She looked at the strange markings and smiled.

"Put the ore back in the slot Angus, if you please" the dragon told him.

Pyrra closed her eyes and started to growl strange noises. Angus recognised the sounds as something similar to the ones he heard when Pyrra spoke to Nathair. No sooner had she finished chanting in the dragon's strange language, when a tremendous bang announced that the doors would be opening; magically, they started slowly and creakingly, to do so.

Inside they could see a vast cavern, which seemed to be at the end of a long corridor and was lit throughout by flaming torches. The corridor was about the height of Pyrra and twice her width. In the distance, at the far end, they could see what looked like a large birdcage. On one side were bars and on the other was an enclosed cave-like section that they could not see into. It was suspended from the cavern by a large chain that held it about ten feet from the floor. The roof of the cavern seemed to be very high and the other end of the chain could not be seen. They heard the terrible growling howl again and this time they could tell it was coming from the cage. Pyrra growled back, but ominously, no sound returned.

They moved forward, looking about them at the panelling on the walls of the corridor. It was similar to the panelling in the castle above them, complete with Celtic symbols. Suddenly Pyrra stopped.

"This all seems to be very easy," she said, "Too easy! My instincts are telling me to stay calm and tread carefully."

Pyrra stared at the walls intently and at the tiled floor. Angus wondered what was worrying her so much, the tiles were just large blue and green diamonds but not in any kind of uniform pattern. They looked totally random, almost like they had been placed without much thought. Pyrra stretched out her front leg and carefully placed her claws on the squares in front of her. Nothing happened. Miss Puttick let out a large breath that she had been holding for ages.

"What's wrong with you Pyrra?" asked Angus.

"Angus shush, let her be. I think she senses something and it's scaring the life out of me," hissed Miss Puttick.

She was so terrified right now that her heart was almost beating its way out from her chest. She tried to relax herself and decided to stay back behind the others. She stepped back and with a speed that almost could not be seen, a panel moved on the wall opposite. A net sprang out of the hole so fast that both Miss Puttick and Angus barely had the time to brace themselves against the onslaught of heaven knows what. They had both screamed out with fright, fearing for their lives! But nothing seemed to have happened.

Dropping his arms and looking up, Angus could see that Pyrra had reacted with lightning fast reflexes and stopped the net by gripping it with her teeth. He could see that the net was being pulled to the other wall and would have catapulted them against it, had Pyrra not acted so quickly. The dragon waited until they had both safely stepped aside to safety and then let go of the net. With a loud twang, it slapped hard against the other wall like a giant spring, just released. Angus looked up and nodded to acknowledge that she had saved them from, well maybe not death, but certainly a severe squashing.

They were less than a third of the way down the corridor and they paused to catch their breath; the near miss with the net had winded them. Angus glanced ahead up towards the cage. They still had some way to go.

"We had better move forward very slowly and carefully," said Pyrra.

"Is there a particular order to the way we have to cross the floor, some sort of obscure pattern?" asked Miss Puttick.

"I think you might be right," replied Pyrra.

"I am afraid that I will be no help to you as I am slightly colour-blind!" said Miss Puttick.

It was up to Angus and Pyrra to figure out the riddle. He thought about the tile that Miss Puttick had stood on, it was blue, and the green ones seemed almost to be a type of pathway that meandered through the blue ones.

"Listen I think it's the green tiles we have to stick to. Miss Puttick stood on that blue one and that set off the trap. The green tiles seem to be a type of path through the blue, like islands," he finished.

"Well that sounds reasonable... okay you two get on my back for safety and I will take you through."

Pyrra began to lead the way along the corridor tunnel, slowly picking her way along the green tiles.
It seemed to Angus that it took ages to move towards the cavern and as they were winding their way through the green tiles, they found gaps and Pyrra had to hop over the blue squares, trying to keep her tail up off the floor. On one leap Miss Puttick almost fell off and Angus only just grabbed her arm in time to stop her hitting the tiled floor.

"I've got you Miss Puttick." he assured her. "Can you get back up?"

"Yes... thank you... Angus," she replied as she shifted her weight. "I don't think my heart can take much more of this excitement."

"Are you both ready to go on?" asked Pyrra.

As they nodded their assent Pyrra began again, moving cautiously on. They could hear the panels twitching and groaning around them, as if hundreds of nasty traps were just waiting for one false move.

So worried and concerned were they about the noises they could hear around them, they didn't notice the next green tile wasn't quite green. It was a blue green, slightly different from the green ones around it, but definitely not blue. Pyrra stepped forward and as soon as her great dragon claw hit the tile, the whole corridor seemed to spring to life. The walls moved; the ceiling shook; the floor swayed and dust flew everywhere. It seemed as if they would be swallowed up into the earth and buried alive!

When the dust finally settled, they were all lying in a heap. They looked at each other as the air cleared, allowing them to take stock of their surroundings and they realised they were caught in another trap. This one however, was as good a snare as you could find. Thick iron bars, that even a dragon with magical powers could not break, surrounded them on all sides. Pyrra looked to the floor and groaned despondently.

"It seems that the other traps were just setting us up for the big one and now we're all imprisoned."

Angus tested the bars and knew there was no way out. Miss Puttick was standing up now and dusting herself off.

"It's no use Angus. We will just need to wait for Rathlin to let us out. I don't doubt that he knows we're in here. He's probably watching us at this very second."

"I think I can get through these bars," said Angus.

"But you'll get stuck and then what will we do?" replied Miss Puttick, but Angus was already squeezing his wiry frame through the gap between the bars and, with a final grunt, he was through.

"Fantastic!" shouted Pyrra. "You must try to find a lever of some sort to release Miss Puttick and myself from this thing."

Angus trod carefully, but he need not have worried as the traps had all been sprung. He looked on the walls for a release mechanism and as he did so his gaze was drawn to the cage hanging in the gloomy cavern. Something stirred inside as he watched and a blue dragon wandered out of the enclosed section towards him, making the cage gently sway on its chain. They had indeed found Cyru!

"What's all this noise about? Can't an unhappy dragon mope in depression without all this interruption?" it whined. The dragon looked down, saw Angus, and sprang back on its haunches.

"Who on earth are you?"

Angus jumped back a step, but then pointed to Pyrra who explained in hasty dragon, why they were here and how it all came about.

"Hurry!" shouted Miss Puttick. "We don't have much time and I think I hear someone coming!"

Cyru pointed over to the left of the cavern.

"Over there, feel for a lever in the wall and release the others."

Angus ran over, but just as he did, a familiar voice rang out like a pistol shot.

"Stop right where you are, or my dogs will attack you!"

Angus froze, as out from the corner of each eye, on either side of him, he could see two huge hunting dogs baring razor sharp teeth towards him. The man that had shouted walked into view and caused a chill to run down Angus' spine. It was Rathlin Tek. He motioned the dogs to sit beside him, blocking the lever. The dogs still bared teeth that would surely rip Angus to bits in seconds. He had never been so scared in all his life!

"So Angus we meet again. Just what did you hope to achieve here?" He paused for an answer and since Angus did not seem able to speak, he continued, "Did you think that I was stupid? Did you really think that you could just waltz in here and take my dragon?" He pointed at Pyrra, "And would this be the dragon you denied seeing?"

Angus stepped backwards as Rathlin advanced. The dragons and Miss Puttick shouted protests from their cages as he did so.

"Look Angus, look at your friends. They cannot help you now" He advanced further. "I've been watching and waiting for you. I knew you would come. Did you not stop to think, when you found my front door open, that it was a trap?" he mocked.

"Why don't you dragons breathe fire on him or something?" Angus shouted.

"Be quiet, they are powerless," replied Rathlin as he grabbed Angus roughly by the arm. "The cages have a dragon spell on them. My dear late brother was kind enough to leave behind some of his findings, which helped me enormously and led me to Cyru"

Rathlin pushed him forcefully and released the hold. Angus, finding himself off balance, fell to the floor.

"And now I must thank you... you have brought me another dragon for my collection," said Rathlin, turning to grin in Pyrra's direction. Pyrra howled in impotent rage.

"So dragon, you wish to harm me. Go ahead and try. Try to breathe fire on me," taunted Rathlin as he walked to the side of the cage which held her. Pyrra roared as she wanted to lash out at the man who had hurt her friend.

Angus noticed that the dogs had moved beside Rathlin, which left the lever unguarded. Slowly he started to edge himself up and backwards towards it. If he could just get a little closer, he could grab it before the dogs reacted and possible free Pyrra. Angus stopped when Rathlin glanced around, however he relaxed again when the man turned back to Pyrra and resume his taunting. Judging himself to be close enough, Angus jumped up and ran for the lever which was still several metres away. That was when the dogs both lunged. They bounded across the cave in no time at all, both pouncing on Angus' back and knocking him headlong to the floor. Each dog grabbed hold of a jaw full of, luckily not Angus, but the hood of his top. They wrestled with it, shaking their slobbering heads from side to side as if the garment was a prized bone, with Angus terrified in the middle. He was waiting for the moment the vicious teeth sank into his flesh, bracing himself, sure it was about to happen and feeling powerless to stop the attack as tearing noises emanated from the cloth. The dragons roared, Miss Puttick screamed and Rathlin shouted orders at the dogs. Somehow amidst the cacophony Angus' sense of survival kicked in and he realised that he could get his hooded jacket off.

He wriggled and moved, allowing the dogs to wrestle the garment away from him. Angus shuffled and backed away from the dogs, not even daring to breathe for fear of drawing their attention.

He was just beginning to think that he had got away with it, when the dogs stopped their frantic tug of war with his jacket and turned to look at him. They both had that mad dog look about them and Angus felt helpless as they began to stalk slowly towards him. That was when he realised that Rathlin was shouting at the dogs. Not to attack, but calling them to heel.

Rathlin strode past Angus and producing a couple of leashes from his jacket, he chastised the dogs, forcing them to cower under their master's wrath. He walked the now timid animals over to the lever and tied them to a metal loop in the rock, before turning back to Angus.

"Are you alright lad?" he asked with concern.

"I… I'm fine… thanks," he replied shakily, but surprised by Rathlin's behaviour.

"I am sorry… the dogs were never meant to attack you… just frighten you."

Angus picked himself up and retrieved the hooded jacket that had saved him from a mauling. He glanced up at Rathlin trying to work him out. Why had he called off the dogs? It surprised Angus that the man he had thought of as evil and uncaring had come to his rescue, saving him from certain harm. Angus could sense something different in the man and he was starting to think that maybe they had misjudged him.

"They could have killed him!" growled Pyrra from her prison.

Rathlin walked back towards the irate green dragon.

"No, no… I wouldn't have allowed that," assured Rathlin almost pleadingly as he walked towards her cage.

Suddenly a hand rose up and struck Rathlin so hard on his face that he was sent reeling backwards. Miss Puttick was not restrained by any magical powers and despite her fear of the dogs she had slapped a surprised Rathlin, very hard indeed, around the face.

"You wicked man, how could you? He is just a boy and you are a bully." She nursed her hand, sore from the force of the blow. "How can you be so cruel?"

Angus watched Rathlin and was desperately trying to make sense of what had just happened. He sensed that their captor was possibly not as bad as they had first thought and he wanted to say something that would persuade him to release the dragons.

'Of course... the PAMPHLET!' he thought as he grabbed his backpack from inside the cage.

Whilst Rathlin was still soothing his smarting cheek, Angus approached him and began to read.

"The Oath of the SSDP is simple. A dragon protector shall dedicate himself to the motto and beliefs of the SSDP." He had Rathlin's attention now, "Respect the SSDP rules of secrecy... Never misuse the SSDP." He looked at Rathlin as he said this, he already knew the words by heart. "Always put dragons before himself and his own well-being and will only pass on the legacy to those worthy of the task."

Rathlin turned slowly towards Angus as he had spoken. The tall man was still rubbing his sore face but he said nothing. In truth while he had listened to Angus, the lad had reminded him of his late brother Finian at that age.

He looked thoughtful for a moment and then Rathlin spoke.

"Is that the secret message from my brother, the one you found?" he said softly, "Is it supposed to make me feel sorry?"

Angus was disappointed, it wasn't working.

"There is a lot more to it than that, but didn't you listen to what Angus said?" interjected Miss Puttick.

"I heard the words. I know the words. The Tek family has followed these rules for centuries. We wrote them," he sighed.

"Then why are you doing this?" she asked, her tone softening.

"Why? You ask me why. Then I shall tell you. The real legacy of the Tek family was the Society, passed on from father to son for generations. We were twins Finian and I, not identical, but twins no less. He was my elder brother by no more than three and a half minutes. Three and a half minutes!" Rathlin raised his voice again and the dogs sat alert. No-one moved or even dared breathe.

"That was all that separated my brother and I, but it might as well have been three hundred years," he continued. "While I was overlooked by my father, Finian was taught all of the secrets of the Society. He was groomed to take over from my father as the head of the order. Our mother had died when we were young and I was ignored, left to do as I pleased, as long as I didn't interfere with their precious dragons."

The venom had gone from his voice. He had stopped talking and paced across the floor to Cyru's cage where he looked up at the captive blue dragon.

"All I wanted to do was look after a dragon. Just a little dragon would have been good enough," he paused as if thinking about a past memory. "I left Calmor as soon as I was old enough and didn't come back."

"Didn't your brother try to contact you or involve you in the Society once he took over?" asked Miss Puttick her voice showing a hint of sympathy.

"No he didn't, at least not until recently. He wrote to me trying to say he was sorry about our inability to get on and telling me that he was going on a long trip. He said he realised that father had not been fair and that he wanted my help. Of course being hot headed I didn't answer and he travelled to the Black Sea and never returned."

Rathlin did not speak for what seemed like ages, obviously anguished by that memory. Finally he continued,

"When they told me that Finian was dead, I was stunned. He was my twin after all and even though we were estranged for all those years, I still grieved for the only family I had left. Then I realised that Calmor, Long Reach and all of the family treasures were mine, but none of that was of any interest to me. All I wanted was the knowledge that had been denied me all my life, the secrets of the Society and the power of the dragons! I thought it would bring me happiness and fulfilment in my life."

He walked up to Angus.

"You are very much like my twin brother."

Rathlin turned back towards Miss Puttick.

"Then I began to search through the notes and documents Finian had left. They were a mess and it took me almost two years to find what I needed. I started to visit the dragons and ask them to come to Calmor with me, but they would not answer. Then I see you lad, at my home, my home, with a dragon." He turned to Pyrra with a look of longing in his face. "Why is it a young boy can persuade a dragon to do his bidding and yet I cannot?"

"Did you not hear the words that Angus read?" replied Miss Puttick.

"I already told y…"

"I know you already know them, but have you understood them?" she shouted back.

"I…I…of course I do," he replied hesitantly.

"Never misuse the SSDP," she replied. "What would Finian say to you now, if he could see what you have done with your knowledge?" She continued, "Always put dragons before himself and his own well-being. How can you be following that, while you have poor Cyru locked up against his will, can't you see he is miserable?"

She glared at him and Angus had never seen her so angry.

"A PROTECTOR will only pass on the legacy to those worthy of the task. Why do you think your brother never passed on the knowledge to you? Certainly your father had a hand in that at first, but then you went away. He could never have known you were longing to be part of his legacy. He has been searching for help for years. He needed protectors to look after the dragons. He would have loved to have had you at his side. Of that I am sure. Read his letter if you don't believe me, go on, read it."

Angus held out the pamphlet and Rathlin reached out and took it. He could see Rathlin's hand tremble as he read the letter from Finian. After a few moments he looked at Angus, his eyes were filling up.

"How could I have been so stupid? If only I had spoken with him before he went. Maybe he would have stayed and we would be together now."

"Don't you see now that Finian was as much a victim of your father's judgement as you were?" put in Miss Puttick.

"I am so ashamed. I have let him down so badly and now I can never tell him I am sorry, or prove myself to him," he cried.

"Yes you can," replied Angus. "All you have to do is release your captives. If you can do that then you will prove yourself to be worthy of Finian's trust and the Society which is yours by right."

"I only wish that I'd had your wisdom young man. My brother would have been very proud of you." Rathlin held out his hand to the boy. He removed the dogs from the chamber then, stepping over to the cage, he freed Cyru.

Chapter 12

'A Curious Thing'

Rathlin released Pyrra from her cage and she met Cyru in the middle of the chamber. They seemed to hug and, after a brief exchange of words that nobody could understand, Pyrra turned to Rathlin.

"Are we free to go now?" she asked Rathlin.

"Yes you are. I would like you to stay, but I don't think you will want to somehow" As he said this, he had waved his hand in the direction of the cavern above them. Angus noticed the niches now for the first time. They were all over the cavern, right up to the top. Small caves! Not too big, but just the right size to hold a dragon. Pyrra followed his gaze and said softly,

"Now I have realised why this place seems so familiar to me… the cavern and the niches around the walls… we dragons used to come here many centuries ago. We came for the Blue Dragon Fire, but also as a sort of visiting place, where dragons could get together in secrecy and safety. That was before the Great Hibernation though."

Miss Puttick had been silent since Rathlin had released the dragons, but now put a comforting hand on the chastened Rathlin's shoulder.

"Don't you think that there is something you can do to honour your brother and to resurrect the SSDP?" she asked gently.

Rathlin looks up at her. He was truly ashamed of his deeds and could see no way to make amends to these noble beasts. He would dearly love to be able to take part in preserving their wellbeing, now that he could see the folly of his previous ways.

"Calmor used to welcome dragons didn't it?" she continued, then realising he was not catching her drift "Well you're the owner, so why can't you do the same now?"

"Now there's a thought!" said Angus enthusiastically to Rathlin who had visibly brightened and no longer looked like a condemned man.

"You can allow dragons to come and visit for recreation in the grounds!"

"What a marvellous idea!" enthused Miss Puttick, who was glad that someone picked up her hint. "Mr Tek what do you think?"

"Well I suppose that's possible, if the dragons would want to come here... it would put to rights, some of the wrongs I have done to my brother's memory and I would get to see the dragons." His angular face broke into a half smile changing his appearance totally. "They would be welcome as my guests and not just kept for my own selfish pleasure!" he promised eagerly.

"That's settled then!" said Angus. "Pyrra you can spread the word amongst your dragon friends."

"Yes Pyrra, if you can forgive me. Tell them that Calmor Castle will once again be a sanctuary for dragons, to come and go as they please, to enjoy the Blue Dragon Fire in seclusion and privacy, under the protection of the Secret Society of Dragon Protectors and led by the castle's owner. You have my solemn word as a Tek on that."

"...and assisted by Angus Munro and Aurora Puttick" added the librarian clapping her hands together like a schoolgirl.

They made their way back up to the castle and Rathlin fetched something to drink. They toasted the rebirth of the Society and then Rathlin stood up.

"I have one last request to make," he turned to Angus, "It would do me a great honour Angus and give me immense pleasure if you would be the first official recruit of the newly re-formed Secret Society of Dragon Protectors?"

"Really, me, a proper dragon protector?" the boy was overwhelmed.

"I can think of no other that I would rather have and who else but you can look out for Pyrra, and be her friend?" he finished.

"Well Angus what do you say?" smiled Pyrra.

"Of course I want to do it! I've thought, and dreamt, of nothing else since I found the letter and met Pyrra."

"Excellent!" exclaimed Rathlin. "I truly wish my brother had known you… he would have thoroughly approved."

"Maybe we can find that mysterious dark green dragon together!" said Angus excitedly.

The new friends stayed a little while longer, making plans for the future and then Pyrra took Cyru outside to test his wings and see if he was up to the long flight home. He seemed to be fine and Miss Puttick enjoyed a nice cup of Earl Grey tea before she said goodbye to Rathlin. Angus noticed that they had got on extremely well and they reminded him of how the dragons at the church had acted around each other. She promised to be in touch very soon, to help Rathlin make some plans for the secret dragon sanctuary at Calmor and she was very interested in helping him sort out the vast amounts of information that Finian had collected. 'Adults, I'll never understand them' he thought.

Angus and Miss Puttick climbed on Pyrra's back once more and they journeyed homeward, with Cyru flying just beneath them.

They saw him safely morphed back into the pub sign and then returned Miss Puttick to her library. The librarian and dragon said their goodbyes after what had been an emotional day. Angus promised to visit her in the library the next day.

"Now to get you home Angus."

"PLEASE, can we just fly around for a little longer? I would love to go higher and faster than you have ever done before. Then you take me home and go back to your plinth in the High Street" begged Angus hoping the plinth comment would convince her.

"I don't know Angus… it's been a long day."

"C'mon Pyrra, show me what you can do!" he pleaded. Pyrra beat her wings harder and faster at this request.

"Okay Angus, hold on to your pants!" she roared before she took a deep breath and turned the speed up a couple of gears. Dragon and boy climbed through the sky, thrusting upwards through the endless white billowing barrier of the clouds. Pyrra levelled out and they were so high that Angus believed he would never hit the ground if he fell off now. He looked around at the sky and all he could see in every direction was a blanket of cotton wool, with clear blue skies above.

They flew for some time and watched the sun turn the blue sky into shades of orange, pink and red setting the clouds on fire.

"Wow it's fantastic Pyrra!" shouted Angus.

One minute, they were above the marshmallow clouds, that looked as if they could take your weight if you decided to go for a walk on them, and the next they were spiralling downwards in a sort of freefall; leaving behind a misty dream world above, that you only ever see from the comfort of a plane seat.

"Exciting enough for you?" shouted Pyrra over her shoulder. Angus thought his heart would burst.

"This is seriously wicked! What a buzz!" he shouted back.

He gasped, fearing for his life, as they seemed to aim for a mountainside that had sprung up out of nowhere right in front of them. He thought Pyrra was playing 'chicken' and was taking it all a bit too far! Suddenly Pyrra pulled up sharply, swept up the mountainside and over the peak. Angus left his stomach behind and his heart was in his mouth. She spread her wings wide and glided down the other side towards a narrow gorge. Angus looked in wonder as what seemed to be a solid rock face turned out to be an illusion. It contained a cave entrance that looked natural, but somehow sculpted at the same time.

Pyrra dropped gently onto the ground in front of the entrance and began to edge her way cautiously inside. Angus climbed down off the dragon's back and followed her. It was quite dark and he could see nothing. He started fumbling in his backpack for his torch, but Pyrra told him to wait and stand back. She took a deep breath and burst flames into the cave. Suddenly the interior was flooded with light; at first from the blinding light of dragon's flames, but as they died down, the light seemed to come from within the rock itself. Pyrra had engulfed a boulder in the centre so intensely that a superheat was radiating back, bathing the inside with an orange glow. This gave warmth to the interior and made it seem cosy and welcoming.

"This is, or was, my home, Angus. I wanted to keep this as a surprise. With Godroi's help, I managed to remember how to get here. Hopefully one day I can come back here to live again when the world's a better place."

Angus privately, and rather sadly, thought that the cave might remain empty for a very long time, but he kept these thoughts to himself.

As his eyes grew accustomed to the eerie light coming from the fired rock, he could see that the cave was filled with stalagmites and stalactites of every shape and size. It was one of the most beautiful places he had ever seen. He wandered around, touching the strange rock formations and was, quite literally, speechless. Pyrra smiled her dragon smile at his wonderment.

"Now Angus, it really is time that we both went home."

"Not quite" he said as he pulled off his backpack and began to unzip it. Pyrra looked on as he rummaged around for something in the half-light. His fingers closed around a familiar object and he pulled an old book out.

"It will have to be re-written now," chuckled Angus, "but I thought you might like to hear your story."

"Yes PLEASE," exclaimed Pyrra. "I meant to ask you about that before, but completely forgot with all the excitement."

As the dragon nodded her assent, Angus sat on a large rock and opened the book. With Pyrra gently resting a green claw on one shoulder and her dragon face peering closely over the other, she listened to him reading 'The Dragon's Tale'.

"It was a curious thing…"

Glossary

Alter-shell - An inanimate object in which a dragon hides. The object stays the same even if the dragon is not hiding within it.

Dragonore - The precious stone which enables dragons and dragon protectors to recognise each other.

Dragon time – A power used by a dragon to speed up or slow time.

Great Hibernation – The name used by dragons to describe their enforced hiding until such a time they deem the earth a safe place to once again inhabit.

Morphing or to morph – A verb used by dragons to describe their transformation into an inanimate object.

Eejits – A Scottish term used to describe an unintelligent person.

Dinnae fas yersel wummin – A Scottish expression meaning fuss or worry. As in 'do not worry yourself woman'.

Thon – A Scottish word for 'those'.

 Debi Evans is a firm believer in dragons. She originally perceived 'The Dragon's Tale' as a picture book short story for young children until she asked John to illustrate it. In him she found a dragon soul mate who suggested a better ending, which turned out to be a beginning. The plot grew as ideas flew backwards and forwards into the collaboration 'The Secret Society of Dragon Protectors' has become. The short story was written for her parents; Joan James who would have loved to own the sweet shop and John James who would still bring the oilcan and paint.

 John MacPherson lives with his family in Dubai and works far too many hours! Born in Glasgow and working as an engineer in the Shipbuilding / Oil & Gas construction industry for more years than he cares to remember, he did not expect to find himself co-writing and illustrating a children's book. However, after meeting Debi as a leader in the Scout movement, she did the unthinkable and dared to open the door to his imagination. Little did Debi know what she was unleashing and together they have created the fantastic dragon filled world that is the SSDP.

Look out for other books in the series

THE SECRET SOCIETY
OF
DRAGON PROTECTORS

'The Cor Stan'
'A Shadow in Time'
'The City Guardians'
'The Silver Claw'

For further details visit the official SSDP
website at

www.thesecretsocietyofdragonprotectors.com